After the Fireworks

PROSE SERIES 9

RAYMOND FILIP

After the Fireworks

Guernica

Printed in Canada.
Typeset by Atelier LHR.

Earlier versions of these stories appeared in the following places: ''Chantal'' was first broadcast on *CBC Anthology* (August 11, 1979), then re-broadcast on *Once More From The Top* (October 5, 1979); ''The Best Ice In Quebec'' in *The Queen's Quarterly* (Autumn 1978, Vol. 85, No. 3); ''Winter Of Content'' in *Quarry* (Autumn 1978, Vol. 27, No. 4); ''Allophone'' in *Montreal Review* (Fall/Winter 1979, Vol. 1, No. 2); ''Rat Racist'' in *Matrix* (Winter 1981, No. 12); and ''Walking On Cried Rivers'' in *Fiddlehead* (January 1983, No. 135).

Guernica Editions, P.O. Box 633, Station N.D.G.,
Montréal (Québec), Canada H4A 3R1

Legal Deposit — 1st quarter
Bibliothèque nationale du Québec & National Library of Canada

Canadian Cataloguing in Publication Data
Filip, Raymond, 1950-
After the Fireworks
(Prose series; no. 9)
ISBN 0-920717-34-9 (bound). —
ISBN 0-920717-33-0 (pbk.)
I. Title. II. Series.
PS8561.I535A82 1989 C813'.54 C88-090340-6
PR9199.3.F44A82 1989

TABLE OF CONTENTS

To Fraser Sutherland:
Infamous critic and fabulous chef
who kept my stomach and pockets full
during the writing of these stories.

Allophone

Vincas Zukas read the trilingual poster, nothing in his tongue. The authorities were organizing a street festival. There was that word again: *allophone*. His sister Ona didn't know the meaning of the term. Her husband Antanas couldn't care less. His nephew Vanny, the Communication Arts major in the family, twisted the syllables into a telephone joke. And the sole dictionary in the house was a useless Lilliput Larousse — side-splitter. In this politician-ridden province, language was no longer a treasure, or an issue, just a game, a friendly fight, with neutral corners growing crowded.

Vincas had arrived in Montréal from Lithuania. The USSR had begun to throw out its mildewed dissidents after the Helsinki accord. In Ona's memory, Vincas had remained that princely partisan during the war, catapulted into a Red Army deportation truck, empty hands in empty pockets. Forty years later, disembarking from an Aeroflot flight at Mirabel, his empty hands were still in his empty pockets. The Kremlin issued passports as arbitrarily as arrests. No suitcases, no kerchief full of ancestral soil, no goodbyes, no gifts to bring but himself at a give-away price, Ona welcomed her brother back, a stranger risen from the dead.

Vincas spoke volumes and volumes those first days, weeks, months, in a new country. How the 9-to-5 line of fire in the Canadian workplace was better than fearing your own shadow ploughing cucumbers on a *kolkhoz*. How their family cemetery had been redeveloped into a track field. How his beloved son Algirdukas had died from complications following scarlet fever because modern antibiotics and sulfa drugs were unobtainable. How his wife Snieguole had been imprisoned for teaching prayers scrawled on birchbark to children. How he had been press-ganged by Red Falcon recruiting officers into joining the air force because he was skilled enough to drive a car! How he had slaughtered Stalin's son Vassily in a game of chess. (A token revenge for the resistance forces!) How he and fellow *saboteurs* would drop supplies in wrong locations over farmers' fields, or register inaccurate information during frontline reconnaissance. What a comedown it was to shiver handcuffed in the gold mines of Kolyma after having piloted Airacobras in the sky. How even the Lord God Vishnu with eight arms could not have shoveled snow fast enough with bare hands for the guards. How the snowflakes in Canada were dime-sized compared to the crystals at Vorkuta as big as Lenin Birth Centennial rubles! How frozen cadavers were rounded up during spring thaw with iron chains hooked through their chins like fish on a stringer. How his gnarled legs ached from nothing sensational beyond sheer daily corrective labor for thirty five years.

"Uztenka! Uztenka! Nekalbek daugiau!" — Enough! Enough! You talk too much! — Antanas would turn off his hearing aid.

The clock had stopped with World War Two for Antanas. His face hung so deadpan it was funny — as if he were the Gulag survivor! Antanas had ruined his eyesight slaving for eleven years inside a dingy textile company. His hearing had been stolen by jackhammers while paving his soul under Montréal streets on construction crews. Finally, sixteen years at Dosco Steel had rendered him drone deaf. In the motherland, he had earned a respectable living as a master accordionist. Now, the only sound of music that came out of him was the raspy gasp of his snoring like a buzzsaw.

Antanas rarely left the house to go beyond the front fence. But Vincas and Ona often took therapeutic walks together, circling the area known as Little Lithuania around Our Lady Gate of Dawn church. Getting splashed by a water truck was as violent as things got in this ethnic retreat. Post-war refugees had spread westward from Ville-Emard and Verdun toward "nouveau riche'' shelter in LaSalle and Lachine. Hybrid perpetuals made way for new generations of ''immigrunts.'' East Indian flotsam, Oriental Ph.D's, Black Rastabillies, visible and invisible minorities, were scuppered from the Third World. These newcomers also collected houses as zealously as postage stamps. Ona recalled how she and Antanas had scrounged together a hill of pop bottles once to meet their mortgage payments. Yet, even here, reunited with his own flesh and blood, Vincas felt as lonely as a cosmonaut in space.

That first summer, Vanny had treated his long lost uncle to a geography lesson on wheels. In his ''Dreamboat Vanny'' camper, he had taken Vincas on a tour of the islands and gulfs along the St. Lawrence up to the Strait of Belle Isle, then back along the North Shore passing Ile d'Anticosti, through Sept-Iles, until the salt air ended at Ile d'Orléans. Vincas instantly became attached to Québec city. The living fossil of the Lower Town reminded him of Vilnius. Ona painted with her water colors from the achromatic Promenade des Gouverneurs. Antanas gazed at the river with his head who knows where? Vincas counted the 1,2,3,4,5,6,7, church steeples in Levis across the St. Lawrence. While Vanny, his wife Marina, and their twin sons Woofer and Tweeter pretended the ferryboat ride was a pirate ship about to steal their legs. In front of Champlain's statue, Vincas posed for a Polaroid One Step, best foot forward, imitating the bronze grandeur of the explorer. Self-discovery.

It pleased Vincas that Montréal emitted such a European atmosphere, old and seductive and larger than the sum of its parts. The language guffuffle didn't ruffle him.

He spoke five: Lithuanian, Polish, German, Russian, English, and was absorbing a sixth like a paper towel: Québécois French.

French had been the official tongue of the boyar aristocracy in Russia. Now the New World was an Old World too, ready for a global garage sale. The English here called the French *frogs*. The frogs called the English *blokes*. The blokes called the Italians *wops*. The wops called the blokes *Canadianos*. The Canadianos called the Lithuanians *lugans*. The lugans called the French *pranukai*. The pranukai called the lugans *maudit polack*. *Maudit anglais, maudit spaghatts, maudit juif, maudit Paki, maudit nigger black, maudit chinois, maudit yo-yo, maudit ta-ta, maudit poulet*: Montréal was not a mosaic, Montréal was mixed nuts!

So that's what allophone meant: a non-English or non-French Québecker. Vincas thanked Robert Gauthier for the free lesson. "Bobbie" Gauthier was one of their tenants, a *liaison*, and chief interpreter. He worked as a sales rep for National Alarm (not a Canadian Unity group but a security firm.) Vincas enjoyed ribbing him about the incongruities of French parlance.

"Vy you say *une table*?" Vincas stroked the

teak chess table. ''Dis table not feminine. No tits!''

''Vincas, *nekvailiok,*'' — behave yourself — Ona slapped his wrists.

Robert noted that even English dialects differed in Québec. There was New Carlisle (''Gasp, eh?'') English, Westmount what-ho English, NDG (Nice Dirty Girls) English, Little Burgundy ''mutha'' tongues, and the ''kitchen English'' of the allophones.

''In Trois Rivières,'' Robert elucidated further, ''they pronounce my name Bobbie Gauthier. In New York, they pronounce it Bobbie Guitar! And in Windsor, they say it Bobbie Goiter!''

Robert had been transferred to Toronto, only to be dealt ''the Argo bounce.''

''Say something in French, Bobbie,'' Hog Towners would demand.

He felt like a freak in a sideshow. For their entertainment? Or education? Conservative teeth would grit at him politely. ''Go back to the woods, Frenchy.''

Isolated incidents multiplied into ripples of intolerance as he headed toward the west coast. So Robert returned to Montréal.

He felt most at home with Vincas: a man who had not lost his sense of humor throughout a desensitizing confinement as a Gulag ''zek.'' Robert also saw himself as a prisoner of sorts, slammed inside the province as a ''Québécois de service,'' and slammed outside as a separatist.

He was a divorcé, no longer in touch with his wife. They had left each other behind "like a pair of old gloves." Graying, childless, no siblings, parents dead, Robert's pastime was the future. He and Vincas would spend hours over the chess table imagining the perfect system that could rise above the dirt of politics.

But no matter how they mutilated, sliced, projected, stapled, bent, or folded the future, it always culminated in nuclear endgame. How to hold back the sunset? As a destruction camp survivor, fate beguiled Vincas. Robert's interest was more socio-metric: odd times odd leaves odd.

The novelty of Vincas' presence had initially inspired Vanny to brush up on his roots. He had bought volume one of *The Gulag Archipelago* by Alexander Solzhenitsyn: "Ol' Sol." However, wending his way through Vanny's sun patio a year later, Vincas had noticed the rain-soaked paperback under a chaise longe. The bookmark, a Kodachrome snapshot of Vanny hamming it up at a party, bisected pages 6 and 7. Vincas had suffered through thirty five years of hell in the strictest of Soviet labor camps for insubordination, and here was his spoiled narcissistic yahoo of a Canadian nephew who couldn't sacrifice more than seven pages of his precious time to be briefed on how it was!

Vanny's excuse was typical. After all that torture, Ol' Sol couldn't come up with any brighter light to endorse than the Russian Orthodox Church. Vincas and Ona would then criticize Vanny for his job as a co-owner of the night-club ''Le G-Spot''. The free thinker couldn't turn toward any brighter lights than mirrored balls, spinners, and rotating strobes.

''For vat I pay you to go university?'' Ona would blare at him. ''To change records for hippy music?''

''Yes ma, I respect my elders and betters. Yes ma, I lay wreaths at your living feet. Yes ma, thank you for the gift of life. At least you took the price tag off that one.''

One night, Vanny escorted Vincas to his singles bar. So this was Free World decadence? The dance floor pulsed with more exciting man-to-man coverage than a football field. Laser lighting flashed like ack-ack. Every cruising creature was dressed to kill. Tanned, scented, glittering studs reeled off poppers, the bump, the disco duck, to Martian music. Not even in the Gulag had his ears ever been racked like this! Out, out, Vincas wanted out!

So Vanny led him to a punker bar. The Tuesday night crowd was quiet, he informed his uncle. One Saturday at witching hour, Vanny had seen a Loto winner shower hundred dollar bills all over the customers like manna from the sky. The scuffle for the money had shaken the dance floor with bad vibes worse than a bass amp at full volume. Vanny had also dragged some boozy floozy out of the men's room where she had OD'd on enough heroin to levitate a hippo. Vincas took one look at the spoonbilled ticket taker with a green Mohawk haircut and razor earring, and surrendered to the impression that he was traveling backwards in time. At the turn of the century, Futurist artists would shave half their heads and smear paintings, or poems, on public walls with their own turds, nude except for top hats, or a monocle over their anus. This nonsense was older than he. Bah! Vanny couldn't tell a Black Russian from a Molotov cocktail.

Vincas had thought of writing his memoirs. But lumpen pens had beat him to the inkwell. He wasn't striving to re-create the hatchet, he wanted to bury it. The information explosion in Western societies had deadened its audience to shock. A lifetime of persecution under the Red Star of the USSR added up to a millesecond splash in the CBC multicolor starburst. Robert Gauthier remained the last person on earth who listened avidly to his reminiscences. Antanas literally turned a deaf ear. Vanny visited only on Sundays now. And Ona could not be reached in front of her RCA ColorTrak TV watching "The Price Is Right."

A long line of pines: his thoughts. A long line of pines like Québec highways. Singing fool driving alone in Ona's Rambler, his "droshky," just for the freedom of mobility without forbidden zones or domestic passports to worry about, Vincas loved the view from a rise outside of Rockburn near the US border; Châteauguay Valley stretched out to infinity at his feet, so arresting his lame leg lifted off the gas pedal first time he had beheld all that green. The meadows, the rye, the sheep beside a wayside cross, reminded him of his native Šiauliai. This could be Lithuania without windmills or castles. But there was Montréal: a hump in the distance like a giant pitcher's mound. How amusing when he almost ran over those golfers at Varennes. The sign said: DRIVING RANGE. Directions. Dictates of foreign customs. His first time on rue Saint-Denis, every friendly passer-by whispered to him "hash." He thought it was a special greeting, until Ona overheard him say "hash" to a policeman in the park. Ona immediately instructed him that "hello" was the formal word of welcome in these parts. Then Vanny had steered him into the rat-tat-tat-tat-meee-meee-meee-meee-meee-zonk-boink-bam-purrrrrrrrr-blppp-blppp-blppp-blppp-blppp of a video arcade. The pilot in him hesitated to take over the controls of Gorf and Zaxxon and Robotron. In less than 30 seconds, he had failed to save the last human family from extinction. Game over. Insert coin. Try Mister Hero. As a student at the University of Vilnius, he had believed that mob choruses sang more righteously than individual whispers in the wilderness. He had scrapped an oval picture of the Mater Dolorosa off his dormitory wall, replacing the sad icon with the sadder face of Karl Marx. Saddest of all were today's idols: blown-up, close-up, re-touched, self-portraits in Egovision!

Vanny was a case in point. His apartment resembled the fifth floor of Eaton's: toys and records. At least high fidelity endured as an outstanding component of his character — as with his father. Though if it had not of been for the war, Ona confessed, she would never have married Antanas. They were united by the flames of burning cities, not the perfume of freesias. Ona's wedding gown still fit. But there wasn't a sofa wide enough for Antanas. The "dead soul" glued himself to the television all day like a shut-in. Ona would squander her savings on impulsive travel, just to get away, fly to Honolulu without telling anyone, cry in the hotel for a week, send home postcards with hugs and kisses and Hawaiin rainbows, then come home paler than ever. Back to babysitting Vanny's twins, born out of wedlock. Marina's Italian parents practically kicked their daughter out of the family womb. Marina told them this was Canada, not Italy. Ona too felt shame and regret. Vanny had arranged for an abortion. Then he and Marina clamped eyes on the "oven cleaners." They lost heart, but gained two sons. Diapers are disposable, but not embryos. Unborn fears. When the Soviet satellite Cosmos 954 crashlanded in the Yukon, Ona slept with her eyes open and her windows closed. And whenever the Central Army hockey team skated into town, she shut the TV, as if the Iron Curtain were in her own living room. Even Vincas couldn't escape the Soviet bugbear. Hunting with Vanny and Robert in the jackpines of Anticosti one October, the discharge of rifle fire summoned up reminders of his brother Petras, a freedom fighter, captured in the communist pines of Prienai forest, nailed naked to a roadside tree in winter with his testacles stuffed into his mouth in order to discourage other "nationalist bandits." Like a drop hammer on his heart, what hurt even more were the recurring memories of his wife. Snieguole, where was she? In Brickyard No: 1? Not your average milkmaid indistinguishable from the cows! He and she would go to sleep with a kiss, and awake with a kiss, and life was one dream. How assured those moments had seemed then. Hot tears blurred his vision so badly, Vincas pulled the Rambler over to the side of the road just to recover. In the work camps, he had never wept so hard as at the communion rail receiving the Eucharist with Ona for the first time since childhood. Ona would cut herself, and Vincas could feel the pain. They had been that close. Now, she too appeared remote, girlish face turned fey from worries, the course of their lives having led to this. To longing for some hallowed place of peace to call home. To hold two handfuls of earth and say here. Not to feel six thousand miles an exile. Not to yearn for any other residence. But to honk your horn, have a neighbor wave hello, and be accepted as one of them. Perhaps good luck was on its way in this province shaped like a beaten heart. Vincas tightened his safety belt, and sang to himself while going home. Where his thoughts were. A long line of pines.

It was another Sunday. Vincas did not go to church. He believed in God, but not in promissory notes to heaven. Superstitious old *bobas* ran through rosary beads as if shelling peas, while their North-Americanized granddaughters minced up and down the communion aisle like a fashion runway. The Mass was an empty ceremony here. Yet, the Sabbath meant more than just the first day of the week to Vincas.

At dawn, he climbed Mount Royal. The mountain was his sanctuary. Vincas surveyed the morning from the Lookout. He loved the serenity, the domes in the sunrise, the iridescent air. The sky, the river, the maples were lustrous with a commonplace grace. Across the sleeping lowlands, he could see all the way to Vermont, all eight of the Monteregian hills: igneous pimples that inferiority complexes here designated as "Mounts." The entire St. Lawrence valley had once lain under a body of water known as the Champlain Sea. But that was before his time. In the Sunday stillness of the island at rest, Vincas felt at one with himself, and with all things. Topsoil blown across the ocean, who was he but a tired man spinning on earth? The closeness and distances that people kept from each other, all the stories out there formed a telling silence. He sat in a secret clearing, a "coin des amis," where joggers and other bushwhackers would stop and converse with him. And Vincas talked, and showed them around, as if he owned the mountain.

"*Perkunas zino kas cia darosi!*" — The devil knows what's happening here! — Antanas locked the front door, shuffling into the dining room with thistleburrs stuck to the seat of his shorts. He had detected a crack in the foundation of his house. And a plague of "hooligans" with guitars were setting up a PA system in the park across the street.

"Vaste ov 'lectricity," He sneered.

The noise would widen the fracture in his suzerain. His garden wasn't ready for this kind of hoedown. And the park would stink forever like the afterclap of a rock concert.

"Relax, pa. Have a beer. This house isn't some cliffhanging mansion in the Crimea," Vanny cooled him down. "Uncle Vince attracted a bigger crowd that day when he tried to sunbathe on the porch in December surrounded by all that snow."

Vincas could never play that one down.

"This isn't the Gulag, uncle Vince," Vanny rubbed it in. "We're gonna have to send you to Great Slave Lake."

"You should vork for God, or Immigrayshun,'' Vincas retaliated. ''You know vere everybody should go.''

''Lithuanian,'' Marina thought out loud. ''Sounds like a prehistoric rock.''

''Yeah. Lithuanians are always stoned,'' Vanny said.

''You be prehistoric!'' Vincas exploded. ''You have two children and not married! Vy you not go live in da trees?''

''Marriage and madness go together like mom and dad,'' Vanny snickered. ''Mutually assured destruction.''

''Crazy society here! Technology go high high high! Morality go low low low!''

''Who's morality?''

''You bullshit!'' Vincas banged the table.

''Okay, Nikita. Put your shoe back on.''

''Everyone comedian!''

''Gimme a grenade. This is a frontal attack.''

''You younk! You tink you know everytink!''

''Yeah. And you're old and you autograph copies of The Bible.''

''I believe dere be illuminated beink.''

''Hollywood special effects,'' Vanny smirked. ''If you're looking for light, call Hydro Québec.''

''No more love,'' Vincas withdrew. ''Game over. Insert coin.''

''Boring! Boring!'' Woofer and Tweeter chanted in unison.

The twins entered the room in matching Jimmy Dean T-shirts and mirrored sunglasses. The duo plinked and thunked ''Puff the Magic Dragon'' on their toy Pianosaurus. No sooner had Vanny started to teach them how to play baseball on the VCR than Antanas ousted the kit-and-kaboodle of them from his sofa. His pop-a-tube-o-phobia distrusted any tampering with the TV; ever since Woofer had mistaken the twenty six inch screen for an Etch-a-Sketch.

''Vaste ov 'lectricity,'' Antanas snapped, as Vanny disconnected the cartridge.

Robert Gauthier then appeared with a gift for children of all ages: a Wacky Wallwalker Spider, ''a spy.''

The twins kept plopping the eight-legged leaper into everyone's potato pancakes as they ate. Robert was one of those privileged tenants who got fed, and not bled, by his landlord.

Vincas and Antanas and Robert then reposed their bellies on the sofa in stuffed array. They listened to the midday news. Unrest in the streets of Gdansk, Kabul, Beirut: destined to be dated by tomorrow. Vanny situated himself on the floor. The three elder men invited him to share a seat in solidarity.

''Individuals, like nations, are entitled to their own self-determination,'' Vanny vetoed their offer.

The discord on TV merged with the street party music outside.

''*Oi, yoi, yoi! Kiek daug zmoniu!*'' Ona

exclaimed from her balcony viewing stand. "So many people!"

A conflict of interest arose. Everybody wanted to go out — except Antanas: the street party pooper. His gluteal muscles chafed from just circling the house. Ona nagged him about his "uniform," that ridiculous T-shirt Vanny had bought him for Christmas as a gag. Sunday, and every day, Antanas wore the shirt like a sandwich board. The caption read: "Visit Russia, Before Russia Visits You!"

"It's only a street party, Ma," Vanny combed his mussy locks. "Not a grand ball."

"You know what we Italians say?" Marina brushed the snarls out of Woofer's hair like mukluk fun fur. "Curly hair means a hard head."

Woofer and Tweeter began to shriek in stereo; a serious to-do over who would cannonball down the sidewalk first on their Ride-Em-Tote-A-Bout. Spinning a 45 rpm platter at 78 rpm (chipmunk speed) usually pacified them. Vanny: the deejay for all seasons and reasons. When that failed, Antanas' advice was to hit the brats over the head with a child psychology book.

Ona objected to their pet names: Woofer and Tweeter. Fine for dogs and birds, but not your own offspring! The real names of the twins were Jason and Ahanu — not exactly Lithuanian or Italian favorites. When everyone had passed Ona's inspection, saluting her as they paraded out, she led the *opera buffa* of her family out into the street.

The sidewalks had turned into an open-air flea market. Homes were warehouses. Junk that had gathered dust instead of interest in basements was going for a bargain. Jesus on velvet dripping pearl tears, or paint-by-number seascapes of anywhere, were thrown away.

A wagon sold pizzas "à la cart." A Polish widow partitioned *pirogis* from her front lawn. Outdoor tables brimmed with Spanish *tapas*, East Indian *puri*, west end *tortières*, southern watermelons, and home-made wine.

"I think goldfish swam in this wine," Vanny grimaced after a taste.

One small all-dressed Italian male, in a maternity gown, frolicked about showing off his "bambino" — a 10 kilogram chunk of Provolone cheese swaddled in babywear. Soccer balls and badminton shuttlecocks mated in the air. Minstrels wandered. A clown on stilts waltzed with a low-built granny. Children waited with outstretched hands to run their fingers through the hair of ponies clopping around in lazy circles. A roly poly soprano serenaded the crowd on a unicycle.

"Hey, *paisano*! Is that a 10-speed?"

The *fête* was conducted with circus discipline. The street babbled like a language laboratory. A stage was erected almost as high as gallows — and just as frightening. The price of admission was as free as the sunshine. Three banners proclaimed:

POTERE AI VICINATI
LE STRADE APPARTENGONO AL POPOLO

POUVOIR POPULAIRE
LA RUE EST AUX CITOYENS

NEIGHBORHOOD POWER
THE STREETS BELONG TO THE PEOPLE

The stern voice of an Italian padre blasted through the loudspeakers. He listed the events as if reading the riot act.

Gerry the Gunner, local legend in his spare time, started the barrel of laughs rolling. Nobody knew where the nickname ''Gunner'' came from — not even Gerry. Rumor had it that in the last war he had served as a tank commander: the drunk tank. Now the city let him blow the national anthem on a harmonica before Little League baseball games. Even in winter, you could catch Gerry making a singing sensation of himself, strumming his gitbox in the snowbank beside a tavern, home on the grunge. Today he excused himself for having to hold up his pants with one elbow. Some bully had ripped off his Bighorn belt. Spurs attached to running shoes, Gerry stomped out a cattle call. Then he passed around a straw hat for the ''patrons of the arts''. And Gerry's mama had taught him a few chords as a youngster to keep him off the streets!

An Italian combo then tore into "The Latin Hustle." For their next number, they urged the immigrant population to count off with them: "*Cinque Tré, Cinqué Tré, Quatro Cinque Sei.*" Earthy senoritas danced barefoot on the asphalt. Odds and sods sprawled on the grass. Rotund men and women wet their moustaches with chianti. No Gina Lollobrigidas here. Vanny enjoyed teasing Marina about that. The ordinary breed of Italian women were built like Fiats: small, reliable, and economical. Sophia Loren was a Lamborghini: fast, elegant, and expensive.

But Marina's charms turned the band members' heads around. No wetback, or son of a wetback, could resist drowning in her ultramarine eyes. The drummer played Casanova. He winked. Marina winked back. Ditto: Woofer, Tweeter, and Vanny.

Dante, another one in the line-up of primo accordion crushers, performed tricks. He made his squeezebox bellow like a train, chirrup like a nightingale, or cascade notes like a waterfall. He sang with as much feeling as a singing telegram. After winding things up with "My Way," he tripped over the microphone cord, his way.

A fiddle *fidèle*, tired of playing reels in the solitude of his kitchen, whipped up the biggest crowd of his life. He was succeeded by belching Bavarian oompah papas. A German shepherd dog beat the bass drum with a stick tied to its tail. The show was degenerating into an animal act. So the emcee grabbed a mike and rallied the "guitar goons" out there, or anyone from the wandering audience, to come up and act out their showbiz fantasies.

"*Eik grot, Antanai*," — Go play — Vincas coaxed Antanas.

"Yeah, Pa!" Vanny was positive for once. "If you can do the Lawrence Welk-I-Can-Count-To-Four Polka, you pass the audition!"

But Antanas turned off his hearing aid and shot them his most wasted "vaste ov 'lectricity" look.

"Buy him a tombstone for his birthday will ya," Vanny expressed their kindred disappointment.

The afternoon sunlight danced on without them. From an observer status, they watched as happier families indulged in the revels. A mother and daughter high-stepped a cancan without spilling their Labatts. A father and son held a beer drinking contest upside-down on their heads. Hairy-chested Roman brios with bricklayer tans played *briscola* on the grass.

Leaning towers of Sci-Fi paperbacks, on the edge of a curb, reached out for readers. Vincas and Robert browsed through them, disputing whether Science Fiction offered old-fashioned escapism or apocalyptic news.

A hammer and sickle struck Vincas' attention. The "community affairs" table was manned by two women.

"Phony baloney!" Vincas discarded their

literature. "You vant see commoonism? I show you commoonism!"

He unrolled the cuff of his pants, exposing the malformed bone configuration from poorly-healed fractures on his right leg.

"*Comment?*" Puzzled the pressure group of two. "*Y'fou lui. Regardes pas.*"

"My French not so fluid! But *Jesus Maria!* If I be good in French, I teach you good!"

"Vincas!" Ona reprimanded him. "*Ka tu cia kvailioji? Neerzink ju! Ainum nuomo!*" — Why are you fooling around? Don't bait them. Let's go home!

"I very sorree for you, sir," One of the community women dared to answer back. "Is not my fault."

"Commoonists make you see like dis!" Vincas poked out their eyes in jest. "You *comprenez?*"

"*Nous ne sommes pas communistes.*"

"Commoonist! Somevere-my-love-socialist! Same phony baloney!"

"Vincas! *Ainum nuomo!*" — Let's go home — Ona cried out, infra-red.

Deprogramming the two women would be as difficult as convincing an Italian that the Chinese had invented spaghetti.

"No. I sorry for you." Vincas left them.

"It's okay, Uncle Vince," Vanny consoled him. "These Québécois Krupskayas prefer medals to diamonds."

Back on stage, the other show continued. A

Japanese boy blew the midnight out of a tenor saxophone almost as tall as he. A Hindu brother and sister act, on tabla and flute, wove a spell that hung on listeners like a charm. Two Yoruban drummers scared away the pigeons, but attracted the humans. A Portugese harpist thrummed along with buskers who were moving up in the world from the subway.

"Ovarb! Ovarb!" Vanny clapped like a chimpanzee.

Any buildings not surrounded by barbed wire, any gathering of smiling people, was a blessing to Vincas. He sipped his wine with the invincible zest of a god feasting on ambrosia and inertia. The triplet rhythms of a tarantella whisked Marina to her feet. She stole Antanas away as a dancing partner. Antanas was too discombobulated to resist. He swayed in slow motion to the *subito presto* beat. Something was rousing him? The beer? The music?

"Where did you locate his 'start' button?" Vanny bumped into Marina, as he tilt-a-whirled Tweeter on his shoulders.

Marina winked bewitchingly.

Robert escorted Ona to shake and bake in the sun. Even Vincas hobbled with Woofer. Antanas had sprung into life. The dead soul was beginning to hop about like a live wire! No more waste of electricity!

Vanny plied his old man with more beer.

"Here, dad. Stimulate the economy."

Antanas' beet-red face shined with sweat.

Vanny guided him onto the stage and placed the communal accordion in his hands. "Show us how you won over ma!" Vanny fitted his Cool Ray No. 1 sunglasses onto his father's nose. "Just pretend you're inside a rock video!"

"*Ar jus visai paselot?!*" — Have you gone crazy?! — Ona yammered. "*Ka zmonis galvos? Ainum nuomo!* " — What will people think? Let's go home!

Antanas diddled his fingers over the keyboard. After fifty years, his gossamer touch had not fled! He clomped one foot down, steadied himself against an amp, bit his lip, then resurrected polka after polka as if from racial memory. He unloaded so many kablooey melodies that his hearing aid popped loose with busy signals. The floorboards bent beneath his weight, adding extra lift to his elation.

The applause was deafening.

"*Numero uno! Numero uno!*" Vanny jumped on stage. "That was beautiful, dad! Like I don't mean Brueghel, or basketful-of-kittens beautiful! I mean like that was BOOOTIFUL! I'm spooked!"

Vincas compared Antanas to Orpheus. He had enchanted the beasts!

But Ona stormed off. "*Nukankink mane!*" — Crucify me! — She glowered at Antanas for advertising his flip side in public — his first emotional investment in this quarter of the century!

The celebration was a surprise party for

everyone. Xenophobes who passed each other on the same street every day in silence, eyeing each other as suspiciously as aliens from another astral plane, now could at least be considered nodding acquaintances. Vincas balanced a bottle cap upon his head, a "hardhat," tipping it to the ladies. Antanas bellydanced. Vincas did the Twist with the sure-footedness of a centipede.

"Put more philosophy into it!" Vanny gyrated up in the air.

Vincas hoky-pokied up to the two Québécois Krupskayas and kissed both their hands with one smack.

The two women froze, overwhelmed by this sudden gesture of peace in their cold war with Vincas. They smiled broadly as if about to brush their teeth. So innocent, so factory fresh in their romanticism, they were right, but they were wrong. What more could Vincas say, except: "May you own da vorld and not pay rent, *mes pitoux!*"

Outsiders, foreigners, floating labor, polyglots, half-and-halves, whatchamacallem's, all linked arms like hyphens. Vincas, Antanas, Vanny, Marina, Woofer, Tweeter, Robert, even Ona, good trooper that she was, the Italian padre, the somewhere-my-love socialists, naturalized and native sons and daughters, names too long for hockey sweaters, all sang "Amen." Vincas' hands were full.

This is why he had come here! Not to die! But to live! To love: that word bled white which refuses to die. Like water on the moon, Vincas drank in that life-sustaining illusion. The street was a proving ground for his praise.

RAT RACIST

Black Label fired the football at Sam's head. Sam's motorcycle kamakazied past, an explosive target. Other warehouse workers shlurped on diet Cokes and Stuart sugar pies outside the loading dock. Sam came bombing back on 4-cylinder thunder. Again, Black Label missed him by a nose.

''Whatsamatter? I thought you niggers were supposta be athletic!'' Sam dismounted.

''I thought you white boys were all yuppies. Y'ain't supposta enter from the rear like us dirty dicks.''

''Fuck off, blackie.''

''Don't tell me to fuck off, whitey. I'll put a voodoo curse on ya. You'll have more needles in yuh than a spruce tree.''

''Why dontcha rent out yer fat ass as a bike rack?''

''Shove it, man. Go ahead.''

Sam ignored Black Label's dare, and parked

his 1200 cc. macho machine beside Herbert's moped.

“Hey, Herbie! Reach the age of puberty yet? When y'gonna scrap that Hell's Cupid minibike and get a killer Kawa like this?”

“Buzz off. You attract the flies.” Herbert flipped a newspaper page.

“Speakin' a ridin' fast nippers. Hey, El Pee. How's yer sister Mahogany? She a Canadian citizen yet? Had her beaver split?”

Elpidio wished Sam would stop his racial slurs. Every day like a circular saw, cut, cut, cut. His sister Mahogany worked as a secretary in the Tailorex offices next door. She snubbed Sam as relentlessy as he pursued her for a date. The mark of a reject was stamped all over Sam as clearly as a box of returns. He took out his revenge on both Elpidio and Mahogany.

“Hey. Is it true what they say about slant-eyed women? That they got slanted cunts?”

“For your information,” Herbert slapped down his newspaper, “Elpidio's not Japanese. He's Filipino.”

“Japs, Filipinos, Chinks, ragheads, the Paki Peril, they're all fuckin' parasitic twins.”

“ The Filipinos fought the Japanese in the last war.”

“Hey, how come yuh always stick up fer them undesirables?”

“If they're so undesirable, how come you desire his sister?”

“Hey! Watch it there, Herbie Herbicide!”

Sam pushed Herbert.

"You watch it!" Herbert shoved Sam. "And don't call me Herbie Herbicide! You understand English?"

"Okay, okay. Relax, man. Who's side you on? Here," Sam unfolded his scag bag and rolled up some hash. "Let's embark on a joint venture."

Sam wiped his jaw in the manner of John Wayne. "Some a yuz starts yer day with a McDonald's hash brown. I'z starts m'day with some Moroccan Red."

"If Ruben catches you, ffft tt," Herbert made a slash gesture across his throat. "You'll get the rap for everything, from trafficking, to possession, to ripping off the company's glad rags, to fucking the watchdog."

"Cool it, man. Y'know who I bought this offa? Gaetan, our head shipper. The needle trade's drivin' him to the syringe. Today's my last day here anyway. I told the Hebe I'm quittin'. Time for some gainful unemployment. UIC, I see you!"

"Other people need the money more than you."

"Spare us the sermon will ya, Herbie. Just do your good deed and drag on the weed."

"No thanks. I get my drugs from Cumberland."

Keys jangled behind the padlocked door of the rear entrance. The motley crew stretched to their feet.

"*Bonjour mon capitain! Comment vous dingy faites?*" Sam ooomphed his fist hello into Gaetan's potbelly. "Care for a joint venture?"

"*Ta geuele, hostie!* Da boss he's in da building!"

"Big deal. Can't smell nothin' with all the rat poison in here."

"Put it away I say! Da boss he's very mad. Da inventory tell dat somebody steal some more stock."

"That's what the friggin' Jew gets for hirin' misfits." Sam shuffled a pack of punchcards. "Who'd wanna steal Ruben's shit anyway? Smart suits for dumb execs. And hey, I'm gettin' tired a diggin' out my name from the bottom of this here deck every rosy morn. All them Lumumba mumbo jumbo names. You were supposta punch out fer me last time! Yuh black barf nigger!

"Punch yo own cawd, motherfucka. Can't you read yo own name?" Black Label answered back.

"Hey! Who's this weird bird of passage?" Sam slid his finger over a surname longer than the box squares on the punchcard. "Chi Chi Mohammed Rastafucious Rahsaan Brown Noser! Holy Death to America! Is that one person or a reggae band?"

"Oh, dat's da maud' *tapette* dere from Haiti who try and *mangé* my ham sandwich, *hostie*," Gaetan grumbled. "I tell 'im to *souce mon graine*. He no come back."

"Yeah. You're a tough suck, eh Gaets? Fuck! Even Do-wop's card is still here! Now there was a yes man. Yuh heard a the Italian Stallion? Well this guy was the Sicilian Sissy. They're everywhere these fuckin' Eyeties. They stick together like rotten spaghetti. Too bad that bald eunuch from Trinidad who married Francine the secretary had to go and break Do-wop's legs, eh? Remember the way me 'n' Do-wop usta rock around the punchclock? Lotsa Frenchies marryin' niggers now. Shoulda guessed Francine would get hitched up with some cold-eyed Carib. Wife-beaters. All that black nailpolish on her sticky fingers. All them fright wigs. All them rings on her fingers and under her eyes from fucking all night."

"Just shut up and punch in will ya? I gotta go to the can." Herbert held it in.

Next in line, Black Label pulverized his punchcard, then spat on it.

"Hey! The shah ain't here yet!" Sam smiled with glee. "Have to boil him in oil."

A scrawny Iranian rushed in. It was Ibn: the only assistant shipper who never missed a day, who didn't wear denim, who didn't swear, and who didn't boondoggle.

"Hey shah, baby. We operate on Canadian time here." Sam tossed Ibn's punchcard to the floor.

Ibn picked it up, punched in, silently.

"You sleep in a tent on the warehouse roof with yer cockroach cousins. What took ya so long to climb down?''

Ibn showed no emotion.

''When are you New World monkeys gonna learn how to talk?''

Ibn ignored Sam and began to sweep the floor.

''Hey, riceball! I'm talkin' to ya!'' Sam crushed Ibn's lunch bag. ''I know somethin' that'll fix yer yap. Let's do the nutcracker.''

''No. Please. I am very tired.''

''You got balls!'' Sam pushed Ibn into Black Label. ''But not for long!''

Sam and Black Label interlocked wrists, enclosing Ibn. Ibn braced himself between their body heat. Then with synchronized thrusts, like forge hammers, they kneed Ibn, front and behind.

''Doughnuts! Walnuts! Pee-nuts!''

Ibn slumped to the ground, doubled up with pain.

''Now that's what yuh call a landed immigrant!''

''You fuckers!'' Herbert scurried back from the washroom.

Gaetan, Elpidio, and Black Label said nothing — experienced bystanders. They stared back with mobile smiles. Smiles you could slither up to the forehead, or down to the chin.

''Okay, schmucks! What do you think this is? The Holiday Inn?'' Rube Ruben, the general manager, stormed in. ''I want this shithouse to glow like a shrine before you leave tonight. Or else you all get *schpritzed*: overtime with no pay. If you don't like it, go cut sugar cane in Cuba. The government's sending over an inspector here tomorrow. Those guys have eyes like Mr. Clean. And if I catch any of you bums swiping off any more suits, you have my guarantee you'll be in prison uniform within the hour! So look alive! Get these boxes rolling, you buncha mental cases! There's two trucks waiting outside! What's that I smell?"

"Rat poison." Sam smirked.

"Rat poison, my pud. Who lit up?"

"The brain drain." Sam nodded toward Ibn.

"You know the rules." Ruben rhymed off the Tailorex oath of allegiance. "No pot. No boozing. No snoozing. No commie rags. And no clit lit."

He paused for dramatic effect.

"And speaking of clits." Ruben eyeballed Sam's Farrah Fawcett poster. "I'm going blind looking at blondie over there. Keep that smut in your bedroom and off my walls!"

Ruben accidentally stepped on Ibn beside the exit, lying limp, like a coat fallen off a hanger.

"What's this shit here? What happened to you buddy? Trip over your face?"

Ibn said nothing.

"Huh, huh. Hang tough there, hang tough. A nice girl will bring you a nice cheque this afternoon. You can send a pot of gold to the peasants back home.''

Ruben scuffed his heels beside Ibn's ears.

''I'll be back quarter to five.'' He squared his shoulders with hauteur. ''Sharp.''

Ruben swaggered out with his business-as-usual stride.

''Whodafuck does Ruben think he is? Moses?'' Sam scraped his work boot across the call numbers of a Tailorex crate. ''By day the fuckin' Jew counts his money on your back. By night he lights candles in the synagogue.''

''Okay, les boys!'' Gaetan smacked his palms together. ''*Vous avez écouté le boss. Toé là, anglais, prends les* rollers. *Toé, les boîtes pour* Maislin. *Toé, ouvres les* returns. *Toé, emportes les* racks *chez* nex' door. *Après ça, tout le gang en bas! Commencez le maud' Christ de* cleanup *et...*''

''Hey! Hey! Wo! Wo! There tweety bird! What ya tryin' a do? Blow the leaves off the trees?'' Sam cut him off.

''Fuck you, *hostie!* When I say work, you work!''

''Well I don't speak French. I only kiss French.''

''Kiss my ass, *hostie! Awai, nou-nou! Grouilles!*''

Sam belched in Gaetan's face. ''Oooops! *Pardon mon accent*.''

''*Quelle corvée!*'' Gaetan collapsed in his chair.

''Seriously, Gaets. I support you peppers.

You know? Separatism: the Pepsi Challenge. I even pull for the Québec Nordiques, your separatist hockey team. Okay, me I'm a Wasp, a vulture without any culture. But I dig yer female chansonyears. Oooolala! Me and some a the O'Toole's brewed for the country went down to Old Montreal, eh? On that big feast yuh got there for that john: Jean Baptiste. Christamighty, we got so goddamned plastered we started fallin' all over them French broads with no brassieres, see. So we tickled 'em pink with this patriotic song we invented. Somethin' like this: 'Diane Dufresne does it. Pauline Julien does it. Michelle Richard does it. So Anne Murray, show us a tit!' Yeah, you Frenchies got my fuckin' support!"

"*Awai, niaiseu*," Gaetan groaned. "Go work."

Sam French kissed the crinkled mouth area of his Farrah Fawcett poster.

"Mmmmnnn. The inspector woulda loved to inspect her!"

"Take it down!" Gaetan growled. "You hear da boss!"

"Put it in your desk. The twerp's not gonna check in there. This ain't like grade school."

"But tonight you take it wid you. Dis not a peep show here. I am not response-able."

"Yeah, yeah. Yeeeowww! My achin' sacralilyack!" Sam trundled two jampacked racks with dished casters up the exit ramp. "This upward mobility is killin' me."

"*Awai! Maud' sans dessins! Après* nex' door, you go *en bas,* wid *les autres* freaks."

"Yessir, nosir, my big toe, sir. Fuckin' inspector. Betcha he's some faggy Inspector Clouseau type frog." Mimicking the Pink Panther, Sam examined some polyester pants with an invisible magnifying glass, snorting between the legs.

"Or maybe he's the Clint Eastwood type?" Sam cocked a trigger finger over his crotch. "Come to investigate the birthday suits."

"*Saint Martyr Canadien! Maud' Christ calice d'fatigant!* Don't fuck around *hostie!*" Gaetan was short with him.

"Ah, *manges la merde,* yuh geek from Gaspé." Sam tugged away the flawed winterwear.

Upon his return, he and Ibn engaged in another encounter.

"Ow! Watchit!" They bumped brows reaching for the same featherweight box. "Where did you come from pygmy?"

"I am from the Middle East." Ibn stated mournfully.

"Y'wanna know where you from? Bacon hater. I'll show you where yer from! Here, do this."

Sam drew back the corners of his mouth to make a face.

"No. Please. I must work."

"You musn't anything! Y'wanna have a cocksuckin' mouth left? Now repeat after me:

I... was... born... on... a... pirate... ship."

"No. Please."

"Cocoa Puff! I'm gonna have to teach ya another lesson!" Sam mauled Ibn's mouth into a stranglehold. "Now repeat what I said!"

"I... was... born... on... a..."Ibn gagged, "pile... of... shit."

"Good Paki." Sam patted Ibn on the head. "Yer English is improvin'."

"*Gang de fous!*" Gaetan harangued. "*Clods du monde!* If you no want to work, *vas coucher hostie!* Early retirement."

Tailorex had no union, no grievance procedure, only unspoken rules. Shady blanks, for office use only. If you were *pure laine Québécois*, you were warmly treated. Gaetan would discuss "les flicks" or "les sports-sports" with you, or let you fetch him a Coke at the Casse-Croute. If you were *anglais*, good for a joke and a toke like Sam, a sweetheart deal could be arranged. But if you were *Néo*, you sweated with no more pity for you than a swatted fly.

It had taken Gaetan eighteen years to move up from assistant shipper to head shipper. The loading zone was his power alley. Whenever loneliness hit him, Gaetan would ring up his relatives, a daily telethon. First, he would call his wife, then his daughter, mother, father, grandfather, grandmother, two sisters, one brother, aunts, uncles, cousins: the entire family tree a telephone pole! As deadly as a power cable, Rube Ruben would descend on Gaetan whenever he caught him kibbitzing on company time. Along with telephones, sedatives, and hash, Gaetan would ease his frayed nerves by chewing gum, spitting everywhere, and dumping on illegal aliens.

Ibn complained to the coffee klatch in the office building. Cold cups pointed toward Ruben's shut door: "the wailing wall." While Ibn summoned up the courage to knock, he overheard "the Rube" on the phone with the elder Ruben, the "big bobbin," the man who signed his pay cheques. Choice epithets such as "miserable schwarzes" and "Chink carpetbaggers" rolled off his tongue. The textile industry was folding, foreign competition, shrinking markets.

Ruben gave Ibn the glad hand, then the glad boot.

"... hang tough there, buddy. A nice girl will bring you a nice cheque..."

Ibn resented being dismissed as a moron. Ruben knew he was a medical student at McGill. He had just completed his sophomore year. A first class student, Ibn was also an Islamic Marxist: a new weave Iranian. Shah of Iran or Ayatollah Khomeini, arms parity appeared to be the sole equality toward which his country was heading. His parents, humble shopkeepers, had been executed by the shah's militia for tending to the wounds of a demonstrator. His brother was exiled in Bahrein. Ibn considered himself to be an *emigré* as well. He had been implicated in marches opposing the Shah of Iran's visit to

Washington, plus the lack of freedom of speech in his own land. It goes without saying, a renewed student visa was denied him. Yet, better to be a breathing non-person on Canadian soil, than a dead citizen under Iranian dust.

Ibn suspected that Ruben suspected that he was a PLO sympathizer. Taboo at Tailorex. How to put the kibosh on all the masqueraded hatred? The mind and body games? The parts-per- million of prejudice?

Ibn's friend and ally, Herbert, was a Science major at Concordia. They shared a certain affinity. Herbert also hailed from a "low-income family" — the high-income euphemism for "poor." Discussing working class heroes and villains provided job enrichment. Ibn couldn't understand how North America got through a day without one single guiding principle — just TV guide. He didn't find it funny how he had to salaam, eight hours a day plus overtime, to Rube Ruben, Gaetan, Sam, and the system of merchandise justice by which they victimized each other. No wonder the Canadian national symbol was a rodent.

Piecemeal, the warehouse assumed the guise of a renovated rat's nest. Evidence of internal sabotage cropped up everywhere. Coats were shorn of care labels, inner linings, buttons, pockets, and zippers: flasher specials. Herbert had traced a foul odor to a Scottish plaid supersaturated with "French dressing": urine. Elpidio chanced upon a dead mouse inside the pocket of a seersucker suit.

A windowless back room, a human feedlot where a fire had once erupted, was cleared of pop bottles, caps, cans, tabs, straws, styrofoam cups, cellophane wrappers, chip bags, English and French fanzines, tabloids, newspapers, apple cores, banana peels, orange rinds, milk cartons, cardboard containers, Stuart pie tins, bits of crust, crud, dirt, lint, swatches of cloth, a toothless comb, half a roach clip, a ballpoint pen, X/O games on walls, and graffiti. Disorganized labor.

The cement floors of the storage basement and utility room were scrubbed to a sandblasted sparkle. Skids were readjusted, sections repalletized, stairs washed, and misplaced boxes recombined in numerical order like jumbled dice. Sam cremated spiders with his butane lighter. Hallucinogenic dust was the only dust that picked *him* up.

The July heat was so liquid you could almost swim in it. By high noon, the indoors had reached the intensity of a blast furnace. No air-conditioning, the laborers ate lunch in the cool of the basement on top of boxes sunken in from slackers. Sam was always inventing some wacko scheme to break his neck, or somebody else's. As the rest of the gang caught up on their sleep, he rumbled down the rollers on a plank like a surfboard.

"Wheeeeee! You can't catch meeeeee!" Sam smashed into a concrete wall.

"Who sent you here?" Herbert sneered. "Manpower or dinner theatre?"

"How'd ya like my knuckles to make yer face look Chinese?"

"Now you know how Ibn feels when you bug him."

"Hey, what's with the buddy-buddy system between you two? I'll take yuz both on! One hand tied behind my back! Punchin' in slow motion!"

"That's for ham-and-eggers missing something up in headquarters." Herbert tapped his brain. "Defend yourself with ideas."

"Okay, Professor Snotnose. Whatdya wanna know?"

"Where's Iran?"

"In televisionland."

"See. You're ignorant."

"Fuck you. I know it's in one of them hostile environments where I'm never gonna go in my life, fulla mongo losers. What is this? Front Page Challenge? I've seen them yellow-bellied cocksuckers protestin' with bags over their heads." Sam whipped his football into Herbert's stomach.

"You know why?"

"Yeah. They're ugly."

"You're so fucking naïve."

"I ain't nobody's fool."

"One day is the same as the next if you don't have a dream."

"I knew you were talkin' in yer sleep."

''What's there to hope for then? The Apocalypse?''

''Who's lips?''

''The Apocalypse. You know? God as UFO.''

''Aw, fuckin' Jesus. Here we go again! BIG MESSAGE! So how yuh gonna save the world this week?''

''Take off your armor, Sam. The mask of comedy comes off dripping blood!'' Herbert shot the football pointblank into Sam's face.

''Oooo! The kid's gettin' vicious! Yuh lost me in yer warp there, Einstein.''

''Look. You like fighting? Then fight for peace, or human rights, or for a union in this shabby company. Sounds hand-me-down, I know. But labor is the greatest mover of tides on earth, next to the moon.''

''Pffft, unions. They're worse than churches now. If one company goes on strike, yuh gotta keep the faith and sacrifice yer dues for their strike fund. Syndicated goons. Or they force ya to strike in sympathy just cause yer local Jimmy Hoffa says so. Fuck me, I usta think the AFL-CIO was a new football league! No sirreee man, the labor fakers of the world have united. Now it's every man for himself. Fuck! Even sexual unions don't work no more!'' Sam hupped the football back to Herbert.

''How gross! You're still suffering under the illusion that all workers are stoop-and-scoop gorillas like you. You're the exception. People like me, Ibn, Elpidio, are becoming the rule. Even Black Label over there is taking computer courses at night to enhance himself.'' Herbert passed the pigskin back to Sam.

''That chocolate shithead gets confused dialing more than one digit on the telephone!'' Sam chuckled. ''Whatdya know 'bout work anyway, Professor? Where I come from they don't train yuh to read print, just deliver it.''

''Me too, brother.''

''So why you callin' me naïve for?''

''I just meant, like, how come I like books and you don't?''

''Cuz I ain't got the time to read anythin' more than a speedometer! Like I'm tryin' a tell ya, I'm a slavin' man! I've done everythin' from pushin' buttons to pushin' dope. I've done the cabbie trip, the telephone solicishittin' thing. I've lugged and looted furniture for Prime Movers. You know? The kinda movers who get loaded faster 'n' the furniture. I've hauled timberline out in poison ivy land B.C. — Canada before Christ. I've worked on the boats, the big sky-high lakers and salties, vibrators on 'em shake yer feet apart if yuh stand too close. You can fall in the hole or slip under the door with the grain dust on them Speedy Gonzales conveyor belts. Two thousand smackers a month they give ya fer riskin' yer life to deliver corn flakes. Yeah, I worked for United Aircraft before they changed names cuz a that stupid strike they had there. Buncha wildcats smashin' machines high on airplane glue or somethin'. I was in Material Handling, eh? Truckin' in these thingamabobs that looked like candy hats. They'd grind 'em into itty bitty little precision parts. Push! Don't pull! This fuckin' gonzo foreman would always holler at ya, a real smoking gun. So one day there was this chunk a cork missin' in the ground, see. Like the shop floor was all cork, eh? Cuz a all the rattlin' 'n' yellin', eh? So I was pushin' this cart over this hole, see. Then the whole friggin' cargo comes crashin' down on me like next year's Dash 7. Like I mean, I coulda been killed, eh? And the company officials, the men upstairs there, just stood around jingling their pockets, arguin' over whether I should train their next scab or not, and how much it was all gonna cost 'em and shit like that. Yeah, I've geared my ass to day shifts, night shifts, swing shifts, Dixieland shifts! Fuck man! I'm reachin' the age where my contemporaries is escalatin' into middle management. And here I am still pissin' up a rope! Still holdin' job losin' contests with the oddballs at the pool hall. Four months at Tailorex is my personal best. If I can't succeed nowhere else, I'm gonna have to join the armed forces. Blue collar, white collar, pink collar, Roman collar, wooden collar, we're all in the same fuckin' shithole we create for ourselves. So spare us yer new industrial strategy, Herbie Herbicide. I ain't met one saint on the assembly line yet. Pow-pow-pow-pow-power! That's the name a the game. Shit, I ain't scared a much. But I shudder to think what would happen if yuh united all the petty proles I've traded scars 'n' callouses with and let those hammerhead sharks give dictation for a day! I'll take this temporary insanity any time! Fuck you!'' Sam fired the ball back into Herbert's breadbasket.

''You're... you're... you're head is full of hype,'' Herbert fumbled for words. ''The running Snoopydog of capitalism. You spend a few years bouncing around in the job jungle. Your frustrations become factory sealed. You just say that's life, that's the way the coin of the realm falls, fuck it. You don't have the guts to try and change things for the better. So you escape to drugs, or porn, or any kind of shallow shit. You're going to end up like Gaetan. Mahogany told me his old man lost two fingers on an *anglais* cutting machine. So naturally, he thinks after independence French workers won't lose any more fingers! The exploitation will simply be transferred from élite English hands to élite French hands, *égal à égal*. Wall street will still control the wall between the solitudes. And we'll still all be fucked thanks to thoroughbred bigots like you!'' The ball was Sam's again.

''Hey look, Professor Left Brain-Right Brain. The left hand washes the right hand.'' Sam wrung his hands in both pockets simultaneously.

''That's deep, Sam. How dark is your dark side?''

''Stick a flashlight inside your head first.''

''It's yours I'm worried about.''

''What about mine? Just cuz I ain't no Stepin Fetchit, it don't mean I'm a Hitler or somethin'. I'm just a regular guy. I like my gas regular, my cheques regular, and my sex regular! Sure, I get a kick out a harassin' dermizip lips like the shah here. But I'm just breakin' in these immigrants, the gimme gimme brigades, buildin' character 'n' biceps. You know, underdeveloped nations. Yeah, life is a rat race. Fastest rat wins. Losers weepers.''

''It'll all catch up to you, Sam.''

''Aw, fuck these unpaid political announcements! If you're a disgruntled worker, write to Dear Abby!''

''Ball of confusion.'' Herbert heaved a sigh.

''Yeah. Ball of confusion.'' Sam threw a bullet pass into a ruckus of Tailorex boxes.

Every Thursday, around three o'clock, Mahogany shuttled through her ''whistle stops'' with the weekly paycheques.

''God I love your bod.'' Sam eyed her with ardor, fanning his crotch with his pay envelope and separation papers.

Mahogany was the prettiest package in the Tailorex outfit. A white camelia blossom perpetually adorned her straight black hair. She had lived in Canada long enough to lose her accent, but not her virginity.

''Hey. Is it true what they say about slant-eyed women?'' Sam undressed her with his gray eyes. ''That they got slanted cunts?''

Mahogany put her temper on hold.

''Hey, you colored girls are supposta be warm and vibrant. I can't touch ya without an ice pick!''

Mahogany scrambled to the next work station.

''Hey! Hey! Hey!'' Sam ran after her. ''Wanna see the angle of my dangle?''

No comment.

''Ohhh baby doll, I'd love to handle your box!''

Sam never worked so hard in his life.

''Scram Sam!'' Mahogany finally erupted. ''You're not my type!''

''Not your type?! Why you swarthy bitch! What type a cock you like to rock with? A ten-incher made a gold? The jock type? Wanna see my hundred-metre breast stroke?''

''Please go away!'' Mahogany brushed Sam off.

''Just feelin' fer lumps, sugar!''

''Okay, you infantile prick,'' Herbert came to the rescue again. ''You got your wad. Why don't you just go home now and jack off like a good little refugee from reality?''

''Best idea you've had yet, Herbie. But first, me and Gaets, we gotta take care a some agribusiness.''

Every Friday, Gaetan promenaded over to the Bank of Canada across the street to beat the rush. Sam was placed in charge during the interim, since no French assistant shippers were on that month's payroll. Sam permitted his underlings to goof off. Relaxing in the basement, they scrutinized each notch of their pay cheques as thoroughly as a CAT-scan.

Ibn got up first. He strolled idly into the stock room upstairs. There, cramming the latest in Tailorex men's wear into four shopping bags, was Sam.

Sam spied Ibn.

''Whatdafuckdyawant?''

''A broom.'' Ibn responded quickly.

''A broom! You're gonna get a big fuckin' broom right down yer fuckin' little Iranian throat! So help me, if you snitch on me yuh mum Muslim, I'm gonna bury you alive under a Gulf station!''

''Hey! What's going on up here?'' Herbert materialized out of nowhere again.

''Your out-of-towner friend here is a fuckin' Nosey Parker!''

Herbert peeked into Sam's shopping bags.

''So you're the crook who's been walking off with Ruben's glad rags!''

''Fuck off, man! Everyone's doing it! Why d'ya think I took this crummy job for? Not to work. To shop!''

''You got more suits in here than a TV anchorman!'' Herbert fingered a lapel. ''It's not even real velvet. It's artificial.''

''Well, whatdafuck do you expect from a

Jew? Even Ruben don't wear his company's creations.''

''There you go again, bigot. It'll all catch up to you.''

''Oh, Hebe-jeebies, I'm scared. Who's gonna catch me? These fuckin' Christkillers don't ask for character references when they hire, or nail yuh to a lie detector test or anythin'. Besides, I gave 'em a fudged-up social insurance number — just to be sure.''

''How are you going to collect your UIC?''

''Elementary, Professor. I gave 'em my friend's address instead of mine. Yuh know? The buddy-buddy system.''

''A dashiki!'' Herbert sampled an Afro pullover.

''Gimme that you fucker!''

''Disorganized labor.'' Herbert shook his head.

''They owe it to me, man.''

''I presume you're referring to corporate rip-offs, surplus value, small medium large and extra large profits . . . .''

''Yeah, yeah. Now fuck off! Soon you'll be doing the same thing!''

Sam stashed the shopping bags behind a garbage heap in the parking lot. At precisely a quarter to five, on the button, Rube Ruben made his grand entrance.

''Very nice, very nice.'' He marched past columns of boxes as if inspecting the changing of the guard. It would have been bad protocol for the big boss not to detect some "petit bobo," such as skids out of line, creasemarks in rolls of raw material, and insufficient crawl space to the toilet.

At one point, Ruben fixed his gaze upon the rubbish outside the service entrance. A vulnerable spot. How Ibn itched to wipe off that smirk on Sam's face. This was the perfect moment. The torrid heat, the strain of the work pace, the stench of the warehouse, the ammonia, the cyanide, the gag orders, the suppressed anger, all finally pressured Ibn to burst out.

"Mr. Ruben, sir. You did not check your garbage."

Rube Ruben did a double take. Cold as a clockface, he gave Ibn the stare. Was that resentment in Ibn's voice? Or mere malapropism? Sam's nostrils flared. He clenched his fists and gave Ibn the evil eye. Ibn shored up his defenses. Rube Ruben waived the incident aside without a word. He and Gaetan exited down a maze of beaten linoleum hallways to the main office. Sam was told to lock up and activate the electronic alarm. Gaetan would return for the keys later.

While the other Tailorex workers cut loose, Sam duped Ibn into remaining behind. Gaetan supposedly wished to speak with him. The only time Gaetan ever talked to Ibn was to shout orders. It was obviously a set-up. Ibn's physical safety said run, his financial security said stay. So he stayed.

When the warehouse was deserted, Sam lynched him.

''So you like to squeal, eh pigshit? Well now yuh can squeal all you want!'' Sam clouted Ibn with a left hook that sent him cannonballing into the basement.

''I'm gonna mince you into ground pork, Paki.'' Sam descended the iron staircase as haughtily as a tribute bearer. ''I'm gonna chop and slice and dice you to death.''

Ibn lay in a state of shock.

''C'mon pigshit! Squeal! Squeal! Squeal!'' He banged Ibn's temples like a tambourine into the cement floor.

Ibn fought back the tears harder than he fought back Sam. He had lived in fear of such incidents, when veiled threats would become real; or of verification inquisitions by immigration agents accosting him on the street; or of SAVAK the Iranian secret police ransacking his apartment; or of the RCMP raiding Tailorex as they had done with DeeDee knit and Brock Engineering where a Tudeh party comrade had been nabbed. But this wasn't the street, or SAVAK, or the RCMP, just Sam. Hemorrhaging, Ibn flailed at the air with his fists. An uppercut nicked Sam on the chin.

''Oooo! You doity rat!'' Sam James Cagney'd. ''C'mon jaundice face! Speak white! Cry! I wanna see the tracks a your tears turn into irrigation ditches!''

Sam tore off Ibn's shirt and pants and

shredded them to pieces. Ibn squirmed on the floor, naked, holding back his sobs.

"That's it! Cry your tender tootsies off! Let 'em hear ya back home in the desert! They'll send yuh a sandbox fulla palm trees."

"Fuck you." Ibn's tongue sprang out of hiding. "Fuck you! *FUCK YOU* !!!!!!"

"Uh, oh. Ttt-ttt. Naughty, naughty. Dem's is gonna be yer last words, camelsucker."

With his size-fourteen Kodiak work boot, Sam kicked and kicked and kicked Ibn in the head until a red mask of blood covered his entire face.

"You're overpopulatin' the fuckin' world you fuckin' fuckers!" Sam booted Ibn's testicles. "You fuckin' untouchables from parts unknown are gonna precipitate a global holocaust!" Sam baffed and baffed, again and again.

Ibn had blacked out.

"Awww, did Sammy hurt ya? Poor little raisin. Shucks. Too bad Sammy don't wear a turban. We could unwrap it and use it as a bandage. I always suspected that's what you numbskulls used it for anyway? But lookee! Sammy's got some nice aspirins for ya! Best adult pain relievers next to sex."

Sam took out a lethal dose of Quaaludes.

"Open up, shah baby! Say ahhh! Say Allah!"

He turned Ibn's prostrate body over.

"C'mon your lowness! You're not being very, ummm, conciliatory. Say Allahhh!"

Sam pried Ibn's mouth open and force-fed the Rorer 714's down his gullet.

"See. This is what yuh call bein' a productive member of society." Sam unzippered his pants and began to urinate over Ibn's body. "Man, I'd love to see the look on the inspector's face when he finds yuh here tomorrow. He's gonna be mad mad mad at ya for dirtyin' the company's immaculate floor. Just like yuh scribble yer additions 'n' subtractions on the faces of our dollar bills. We know it's you fuckin' space invaders. This is what you get for stealin' our jobs. And it's a crime and a sin to steal. Over here in the civilized world, when our skin turns your color, we go see a doctor. Fuck the Third World, you're lucky I don't deport ya to the other world!"

Sam hosed the blood off Ibn's face with his piss.

He buckled up, set the alarm, switched off the lights, and locked the door.

"*Ça marche?* Everyting is closed?" Gaetan reappeared.

"Yes sir! Here's yer keys to the kingdom. Everythin's copesetic, antiseptic, and plain cool."

Sam re-sold Gaetan his two grams of Moroccan Red.

"Dis da good stuff?"

"It's the inside dope, man. I bought it offa yuh last week."

"Okay, fuck off." Gaetan fished out a crisp twenty dollar bill.

''Mercy *beaucoup.*'' Sam tweaked Gaetan's new sport shirt. ''Froggy's all set to go a-courtin', eh?''

''Fuck off! Don't touch! Goodbye!''

''Hoo, yes master!'' Sam bowed, tipping a forelock.

Sam hid in the alleyway while Gaetan backed his Toyota out of the parking lot. Rube Ruben's Custom Continental glared at Sam. Ruben never left his office before eight o'clock. So he was safe.

Sam retrieved his going-away present to himself from the trash pile at the service entrance. He stuffed his new fall wardrobe into his Kawasaki saddlebags. This was going in style. Tailorex was just another memory lane now. His bike had been in the sun all day and the seat *sautéed* his behind. Speaking of the hots, he had forgotten his Farrah Fawcett poster. Fuck her.

''Shalom Tailorex! Shalom slanted cunts! Shalom 18 ft. clearance! Shalom four months of my life! Shalom Shah!''

In the middle of his farewell address, Sam felt a huge slam on his back. It wasn't Charlie's Angels, but one of Montréal's burliest cops. Behind the policeman, stood Gaetan and Rube Ruben. Mobile smiles.

With his business-as-usual stride, Ruben stepped up to block Sam's forward path.

''Okay, buddy. Open the bags.''

Sam gunned the throttle.

WINTER OF CONTENT

Iff ya dont gif me ann A in Frrench I'm guna bern da fuken skool down.

Yorrs trooly,
Fuk you.

"King's English." Mrs. Rosemary smiled. "I wouldn't worry about it."

William King, alias "Wet Willie," had just deposited another "sick Bic" message inside a teacher's letterbox. The communiqué had been scrawled upon used toilet paper, discovered that morning by Paul Ryan: substitute teacher.

"He could at least spell his four-letter words properly." Malcolm Semper, permanent English teacher, parachuted the stinking tissue into a wastebasket. "Quintessential flop."

Paul Ryan could not afford any more risks. The previous semester, all four of his tires had been slashed, and an expensive pair of corduroy pants had fallen upon the classic bubble-gum-on-a-seat prank. Pupils no longer brought apples for their teacher, but Facelle Royale letters sealed with a fart.

Paul padded through the chatter of the teacher's lounge. He tried to belong with pedantic alcoholics, Fémol libbers, blackboard radicals, Vivol smiles, Correctol posteriors, working stiffs. Like students, teachers gravitated toward the coziest seating arrangements: geometry specialists in their circle, Phys. Ed. heads in their team, French whips in their *tête-à-tête*, English disciplinarians in their scrum, chemistry instructors in their husband-and-wife combinations, religion masters in their amen corner, and subs in their subgroup. Veterans knocked off one period per time like slicing bread. Tired youngbloods slowly traded in Castanada and Ilyich for seniority and tenure.

"School days, work-to-rule days." Mrs. Rosemary studied a sheaf of form letters. Everyone liked her. She kept the work-to-rule atmosphere comically relieved. Her students were called "Rosemary's babies." She observed the world through large easy-to-read eyes.

"I don't know which is worse?" she said. "Receiving hate mail from William King, or the Quebec government?"

Increasing workloads, declining enrollment,

surplus of sages, mindless vandalism, cutbacks, closures, declassification, controlled burn-out, a list of grievances as long as the arm of new language regulations: job insecurity was robbing the joy out of dedication.

"It's that blimey BNA Act!" Mrs. Rosemary beefed. "If agricultural zones are non-confessional, then why not school regions? What do you think Paul? You're our resident law student."

"Well, I'm studying criminal, not constitutional law," Paul replied.

"What's the difference?"

"Moot point. No matter how you rearrange the divisions: French-English, Protestant-Catholic, nullifidian or in nirvana, the state of affairs here has become so fragmented that devising a homogeneous pecking order for ourselves would involve the art of the impossible."

"Cleverly put, Paul. I don't know what you just said, but you'll make a lawyer *extraordinaire!* You can leave Quebec for Philadelphia!"

Paul Ryan was in his second year of Law at the *Université de Montréal*. He subbed on the side for both the Anglo and Francophone school boards — his "daily double" with the races. Paul was a product of the '60's skidoo system: ascending up the Schoolbell Curve of higher expectations, only to tumble down jobless on the other side.

What Mrs. Rosemary did not realize about Paul was that he had once been an outlaw, a participating dealer in a drug ring. There's no business like Cannabiz. He had never been busted by a narcotics squad. But a snow-blind contact had almost whipped his brains out with a .22 calibre pistol. As a souvenir, a steel plate protected his fractured skull from the outside world. Paul was grateful just to be alive and pushing thirty.

The mailman had handed him his diploma (major in Political Science). His undergraduate career had been wasted as a pusher of "McGill red and white uppers and downers" and hot psychotropic candy that made your mother come in colors. Then came survival in the legitimate job market. Paul crashed through a one-year teacher certification program, clinched a piece of the full-time wall in a high school, only to be "bumped" in his probation year by the hidden hand of bookkeeping. *Une job pas steady*. His patience bore a short tread life. So through the support of his wife, and supply teaching loopholes, Paul entered Law.

The chaos of his own past attracted him toward order. Be it in jurisprudence, the laws of thermodynamics in nature, serial music, or even Murphy's Law: whatever can go wrong will. Paul countervened with his own amending formula: whatever can go right will. Ryan's Law. It all took time. The sword of justice was not a switchblade.

Paul crossed the lounge to the window with all the light. It was snowing. He watched the snowflakes do their elimination dance, melting soundlessly into the soggy streets. The winter blahs were everywhere. A staff member tallied off dates on the calendar.

"Well, well. Easter's in March this year. Approximately three hundred and eighty two hours away!"

In a secluded corner, a male figure sat knitting.

"Hi, how are you?" Paul smiled, standard procedure.

The misanthrope continued to knit and purl in silence.

"What's wrong with him?" Paul asked Malcolm Semper.

"Oh that's Mr. Crabwise. He just came off sick leave for cancer. The tumor was more benign than him. He's generally a nice guy. Everyone gets a little flakey this time of year."

"I like the tuque he's knitting."

"Right on."

Malcolm Semper and Mrs. Rosemary were the only two people with whom Paul could hobnob after a year of service.

"Incidentally," Malcolm added. "Do you feel like playing broomball after lunch? Teachers versus students. The way some of those sweathogs fly at you, they make more than your nose run cold. Mr. Lapierre's still in hospital after the last barnburner. And the parents are starting to complain about their kids coming home in casts looking like Op Art statues. We're considering just having a table hockey league. Not a very persuasive salesman, am I?''

''Well, if I'm game enough to step into a classroom with those happygators, I'm game enough to step into a rink.''

''That's the spirit. So who are you subbing for today?''

''Lippé.''

''Oh yes. François has been chug-a-lugging more than he can take lately. I don't blame him. Wait 'til you meet his desk hoppers. He's doing book reports with them now. It takes them a whole week just to read a newspaper in English, never mind a novel in French! If you can change their attitude, you can make the snow stop falling.''

''Thanks.''

''Oh, don't let me discourage you, mate. Have fun babysitting!'' Malcolm sallied forth to his next class. ''And if they fall asleep, make sure you turn them over on their stomachs!''

''What do I do if they vomit?''

''Run!''

Malcolm Semper fancied himself a revolutionary for having introduced CanLit into the curriculum, and for being able to operate audio-visual aids without anybody else's assistance. Paul had sat in on one of his Creative Drama sessions. Whirling, swirling, spinning young scholars were smashing each other off their feet. They were pretending to be falling snowflakes. The locomotion supposedly increased self-knowledge. Paul saw their glissade as an exercise in futility. No one hires falling snowflakes. The majority of the students were going through their Sesame Street Fighter stage. These snowflakes needed better direction. As for self-expression, Paul remembered transcribing the rhymes of Emile Nelligan and Dylan Thomas for homework during his adolescence; just as Shakespeare had copied out Horace and Juvenal *verbatim et literatim*. Now, as an articulate adult, Paul never felt cheated of any Mickey Mouse muse.

Discussions about the importance of literacy were greeted with looks as blank as snow on a television screen. However, invoking Ryan's Law, Paul believed words would never lose their way through electronic spin-off. Once, in a French schoolyard, Paul had spotted English, French, and immigrant teenagers drawn together by a transistor radio. They were singing along to the chorus: "Why can't we be friends? Why can't we be friends?" — by a band ironically called War. The scene would have been corny as an ad on an educational channel. But there it was, in real life, and it moved him.

Paul still experienced cold feet as he took attendance. This was the tough part, asserting yourself from the beginning. Benevolent despot, he faced the front line.

"Okay, attention please! Call out your names, one at a time, starting with this row."

"Sir, Augustino Pompeo."

"Sir Augustino Pompeo? We have a knight

in our presence!''

Giggles. They liked that. Laughter warms.

''Next.''

''Maya Tremblay.''

''Next''

''Nabih Chihata.''

''Next.''

''Fuck me! Lippé's pickled again!''

A stacked female student tramped into the room. Two male bosom buddies hovered over her.

''You're late, sunshine. Where's your pink slip?''

''My pink slip! Sir! Whatdya think I am? A prostitute!''

Titters.

''I asked you a question! Where is your pink slip?''

Her breasts stuck out like dunce caps. She pointed them toward her bosom buddy on the left.

''He's got it.''

''I lost it, sir.''

''Liar! Liar! Pants on fire!''

''Okay. All three of you morning glories, go to the office, get a new slip. Now!''

''Wait a bit, wait a bit, hold on, sir. Here it is. Don't go psycho.''

The bosom buddy unzippered his fly. Then, through a hole in his pocket, rotating his hips in simulation of you know what, he produced the pink slip.

"Ta daaa!"

Titters.

The things well-tempered teachers had to put up with in order to uphold Fort Knowledge! As a schoolboy, Paul had never razzed a replacement. Secretly, he sometimes yearned for the corporal punishment of his Catholic upbringing. These immature whippersnappers had it too good. They were the beneficiaries of a dead system. The Sulpicians, who had trained him with dog obedience rigor, had lived on school grounds, were omnipresent, fasted, and never got sick.

Paul could swear this pink slip routine was rehearsed. He uncrumpled the paper, then ticked off the names on the attendance sheet. Lo and behold: a certain William King.

"Uh, sir. They spelled my name wrong. My real name's Wet Willie King. My mother's the Queen of Snots. What's yer name?"

"I beg your pardon?"

"Oooo. He's a beggar."

"My name is Mr. Ryan. And if you know what's good for you, you'll be seated and start working on your book report."

"Book report! Awww, sir. Can we play murder ball instead?"

"How is murder ball going to help your future?"

"Ah, that's easy. My future is to murder and to ball!"

Titters.

''Would you prefer a spelling test?''

''No sir, man! Like we've been tested and re-tested so often I'm startin' a feel like a Timex wristwatch! C'mon sir. Give us a break. Yer supposta be on strike or sumptin.''

''It's known as work-to-rule, Mr. King. And it still means *work*!''

''Awww, c'mon sir. We know you're losin' business cuz a one fuckin' pill, and all the sepratits bullshit, and educashun don't make yuh a suckcess no more no how. You're just jailin' us in longer cuz there's nothin' out there fer us. Then we get fucked whenever you get fucked and the whole fuckin' shit just goes around. Fuck! It ain't fair, man! Fuck, when I graduate, I'm gonna wear my fuckin' grad ring through my fuckin' nose, fuck!''

''Who taught you how to speak like that?''

''Our fuckin' teachers!''

''Well I'm going to teach you how to speak English.''

''But sir! This is a French class!''

''*Parfait mon tou-tou, lequel-veux tu? Anglais ou Français?*

''He's a fuckin' frog! Kill him!''

''Hey, wise guy. You talk to me in a civilized tone.''

''Okay, what tone yuh want? Do-re-mi-fa-sol...''

''Hey! I said watch your tongue!''

''I'm watchin'! I'm watchin'! See!'' William King crossed his eyes and wriggled his tongue. "I ain't afraid of you, Frenchie! See what we did ta the other Pepsi professor? Put his middle leg up in traction with the other two!"

Titters.

"Okay, kid. Save your act for Creative Drama."

Sheep in wolves' clothing, contain the leader of the pack and the flock was safe. William King kicked up a chair, rocked edgily against the wall, feet up on his desk as if in a hammock.

When the attendance was completed, William King raised his voice.

"Hey teach! If yer last name's Ryan, how can yuh be French?"

"Ever hear of Claude Ryan?"

"Naw. Who does he play fer?"

"Okay. You like games? We'll play a game. It's a tug of war between good and evil. I want you to write down all the things you hate. If you hate school, suggest something better that hasn't been tried yet? If you hate the French, would you want them to hate you for the same reasons? I want you to write it in French. And I want you to see how easy it is to say bad things, and how hard it is to praise."

Another awww-inspiring project. Paul's deicing efforts had met with the same enthusiasm in the *Commissions scolaires françaises*. Educators, from Socrates' throne on down, had joined ranks throughout the centuries to deal with mentalities such as that of William King's. The prospect of compliments ever issuing out of Wet

Willie seemed to be toilet paper thin.

The remainder of the period deteriorated into a slow-speed chase between the big arm and the small arm of the clock. William King scribbled on the wall, the floor tiles, the desk, the chair, his hand, his ankle, a classmate's cheek, everywhere but on a Scribbler.

"Hey teach! Yuh playin' broomball today?"

"Sure," Paul answered, patrolling the aisles. "Oughta be a sweep for the teachers."

"Huh, huh. You're gonna eat yellow snow — *sir!*"

Two teachers in tennis shoes, four students, and a caretaker cleared the school rink. Huge gobbly snowflakes dribbled from the sky. The teacher/student ratio that showed up for the game corresponded to that of a classroom: 15 against 1. Four athletic academics volunteered to oppose about sixty underlings. The stubbliest brooms were bestowed upon the teachers. The pupils made do with bare sticks, mops, and assorted conversation pieces. Both goalies defended their nets with scraper shovels. Due to such low-budget blemishes, and other irritants, the lunchtime spectacle was named "The Clearasil League." Teachers participated to rid themselves of unwanted calories; students participated to rid themselves of unwanted teachers. The referee was Mr. Monday: guidance counselor.

That afternoon, the pedagogical brain trust of greater Montréal boasted a fat chance of winning: Hefty Harry Zuckerman, machine shop guru. Hefty Harry's girth was almost as wide as the goalie's net. He was a one-man blockade. You had to drill a hole through his belly in order to get a ball past him. He puffed on a cigar while kangaroo-hopping about his cage with a broom between his legs. He was really three men in one. So that evened up the sides at six apiece.

Mr. Monday blew the whistle. The teams hammered each other so hard that the boards began to warp like gunwales. Students doled out punishment to teachers indiscriminately. Paul was clobbered on the backbone by a bladeless hockey stick. It hurt like a hakapik. He swung around. William King blew him a kiss.

As the game progressed, Wet Willie needled Paul more and more. During one mad scramble around the net, he constrained Paul by the hair, enquiring as to whether he had eaten his "French pee soup?" Archaic slang was still being slung by a new generation of sharpshooters. That bothered Paul more than any attempt at character assassination. The penalty box deterred Wet Willie no more than the principal's office. In a pile-up around the crease, Paul felt the sharp edge of the scraper shovel, like a blunt sword, press into his neck. William King ironed on the squeeze, again. The blade came dangerously close to the steel plate behind his cerebellum. This was more than just Charley Horsing around.

The teachers fell behind as often as Hefty Harry's pratfalls. The students chalked up a commanding ten point bulge. Teachers struggled to catch up with their breath, let alone the score. The invigorating joust kept the blood circulating alright.

Malcolm Semper was sandwiched into the boards, pressed ham, by three cannonading bodychecks. He raised himself up by his broomstick, then scampered for his life, quoting Macbeth: "Whence is that knocking? How is't with me, when every noise appals me? What hands are here? Ha! They pluck out mine eyes!"

The climax came in the dying seconds of the game. Wet Willie clamped Paul's skull into a headlock and banged his forehead splat into a crossbar. William King, weighed down with heavy leather and chains, stood a shade taller than he, but Paul lifted the manchild and walloped him so furiously against the goalposts that the pegs popped off. Then Paul blew his top.

"So you want me to bloody your sweat, eh? You want me to wrap you like a ribbon around this net, eh? They'll need a corkscrew to unplug your head out of your asshole! So wisen up showboat! Everybody's got balls! Now show us some brains!"

Paul let off so much steam it was a wonder the rink didn't melt. Wet Willie shriveled instead. Paul released the scruff of his collar. Both of their jackets had ripped open. William King cast a long long look at Paul. Could the kid see the kilometres on him? Could he tell that he had once been a rebel too, without a cause or effect?

A Sesame Street Fighter.

''Sorry I'm such a hard marker.'' Paul slapped Wet Willie's damp rump in camaraderie.

William King sulked in silence with grudging respect. Mr. Monday held open the gate.

''Well, gentlemen. I guess it's table hockey after this.''

Uncinched waistlines, loosened neckties, stubbed-out cigarettes, dissolved valiums, drubbed faces: it was obviously the end of the day. Paul slouched upon a chesterfield in the teachers' lounge. He pinched his sinuses and still beheld roomfuls of self-starters, kick starters, hyperactive, slow, dyslexic, under-achievers, over-achievers, never-achievers, upgraded, non-graded, degraded, streamed, drowned, phased-in, phased-out, *wunderkinds* and kind wonders, not to mention your average institutionalized high school spirits who enter as question marks and come out exclamation points! Why did he always feel as if he had dropped off every ride at La Ronde right before the final bell?

Now he could snooze. Paul had gone to bed late that night burning the midnight megawatts over felonies and misdemeanors and accessories and damages, only to be dispatched for substitution duty at 6:50 a.m. Eastern standard sleepiness.

Paul couldn't sleep. His hungry stomach kept making a fist. He hadn't eaten all day, save for the processed-cheese-that-tastes-like-plastic sandwich before the broomball game. He sauntered toward the cafeteria. Everything was closed, washed, put away. Only breakfast cereal was available. Paul took it. He may as well begin the day again. He loathed the hygienic solitariness of the cafeteria. So he ambled back to the teacher's lounge, listening to the acoustics of his heels echoing across the deserted corridors.

Paul preferred his aloneness in a crowded room. He read a newspaper for company, munching. War, war, war: forecasts of a third world war before the end of the decade, civil wars, holy wars, gang wars, Cola wars, office in-fighting, family feuds, marriage conflicts, bouts with cancer, racial clashes, sports rivalries, landlords vs tenants, army of the unemployed, and the enemy within! Paul was too terrified to budge.

Three Fémol libbers sat down on an adjacent sofa. His wife had met them at the school Christmas party and had dubbed them: Frumpy, Grumpy, and Dumpy. He trusted his wife's judgment of women. They were discussing their love life, male bashing.

"... this morning I actually contemplated sprinkling Howie's sunny-side-up eggs with cyanide." Dumpy said.

Paul choked on his Honey-Nuts, pretending not to hear. But he couldn't resist catching more snatches.

"... the husband and I are still dragging out our interface in sickness or in health or in wrinkles. My gynecologist tells me my thrombo-embolism comes from smoking while I was on contraceptives. Looks like I flunked my orals. I told Dirk to buy some more of those studded condoms. But they're only available in the States. Honest to God, Claire, I'm dying. I don't know which to give up: smoking or screwing?'' Grumpy said.

Were they twitting him with small talk about their twats? Female chauvinists sounded as dumb as male chauvinists. What did their kind of indignity prove? They were a far cry from his wife Johanne. She most likely couldn't pronounce their polysyllabic Ishkabibbles, and her looks department was of the same lesser school as his, but Johanne could teach them a simple thing or two about love. Vacant moments, love fulfilled.

Battle of the sexes. Paul had had enough of battles for one day. He retreated to his favorite window. Increasing cloudiness and unstable fronts prevailed. A significant accumulation of snow buried all life. Snow snow snow snow snow snow snow snow. The ''snow torture'' Paul called it — the Canadian equivalent of the Chinese water torture — in slow, persistent, cold degrees that invaded the nerves. A grade nine girl that afternoon had questioned him about the morbid snow imagery in French- Canadien literature. Paul had advised her to consult an Inuit. Visionaries focus on Québec snow and see coffin fixations. Ordinary folk dance on the white delight and see *joie de vivre*.

But not today. Gloomsday gray. Empty seats. The absentee rate amongst teachers was almost as conspicuous as that amongst students. One "life skills" mentor had actually told him two weeks in advance when she planned to be ill, and what to assign her class for homework. Paul was a "Resource Person." He felt like a gold mine. He paced back and forth among the chit-chat, staring out the window. Someone had broken their leg skiing Jay Peak. Somebody's five-year-old boy had been thrashed to death inside a snowblower. Someone was grumbling about backaches and waking up in the morning "feeling hanged." Another malcontent sniveled about his vacation in the Caribbean.

"You go to The Islands to get away from the ice. And what happens? The airline loses your luggage. The hotel steals your money. And you get followed by these Jamaican Jackos who insult you on the street for having white skin you're afraid to lay down and tan!"

All the yakking about money reminded Paul that he had forgotten to pick up his employee's receipt. Cash: his reward! The bell blasted just as he ventured into the hallway. When would they install tubular bells?

Returning to the teachers' quarters, Paul noticed a sheet of paper inside Mr. Lippé's letter-box.

Deer Mr. Ryn,

I'm sory I kald yu a frogg. I know how itt feelz. We all cum frum Afrka. Pleez exkooz dis lowsy handritin but I'm riten itt on my soar nee. Thair both soar after da game. Itt was a good game. Hope I seez yu soon.

Sinseerly,
William King.

Paul showed the loose leaf paper to Mrs. Rosemary.

"Good news! Malcolm, look! Paul has good news! And it isn't religious!" Mrs. Rosemary passed the note on to Malcolm Semper.

"I never thought broomball would make a good vocabulary builder. And he put his periods in the right place too!" Malcolm handed back the neatly-written message. "Mind you, it could have boomeranged either way. I mean, you could be driving home tonight with a smashed windshield instead."

Paul tucked the note victoriously into his jacket pocket, beside his Bics. William King's royal pardon would not rate very high upon the Edward Fry Graph for Estimating Readability. But the boy's forthright disclosure honored Ryan's Law to the letter.

Paul hurdled over a snowbank, did a joy-to-the-world cartwheel, slapdashed into the reserved parking space, scooped up handfuls of reserved snow, and whupped the whiteness at the pale winter sun. Paul's snowball burst in mid-air. Instead of ducking, he let the snowflakes shower all over him. When was the last time he had done that? Or even made a snowball?

He checked his windshield: frosty, but still there. Same with his second-hand Michelins — only the prices slashed. Paul switched on the radio and rubbed his hands together like two pistons powered by satisfaction. The music of Maneige warmed his ears. Whatever can go right will. The road was clear.

The snow had stopped falling.

Chantal

The cobwebs were built stronger than the rooming house I inhabited that winter. Furnaces overheated, or never heated. Oilcloth was gummy with oil, floors littered from loiterers, walls so hot you couldn't touch. I speculated there would be a fire before the Christmas rush.

The door protecting my privacy bore the marks of boot heels, crowbars, and bare fists: B & E technology. The jamb was pockmarked with chips and dents from jimmied locks. The wood contained more holes than a Legion dartboard. Above the door, a lopsided window could be removed from the outside. Another "bachelor apartment" beside mine housed no display window above the door — but two bullet holes stared back dead center.

Warnings were scotch-taped over peepholes: pay the rent in cash every week, keep the shared bathroom clean, don't dry clothes on the heater, don't switch on the lights during daytime, and dispose of garbage via the back shed. But the shed had no steps! A black pitfall, Mondays and Thursdays, Glad Bags and greasy boxes skydived three storeys like home-made bombs.

The décor was strictly Louie the 14th: if you didn't pay Louie by the 14th, he kicked you out. Chairs: Salvation Army *nouveau*. Kitchen table: arborite with a floral design created by cigarette burns. Pinewood desk: inlaid with swastikas and FLQ initials (early provincial). Hide-a-bed of nails, screws, and mattress coils: sight unseen. Plus a dresser with a mirror that wasn't cracked, warped, or flyspecked. Knock on glass.

For what it lacked in style, the building more than made up with characters who called it home. The day I brodied in with my books, and more books, I confronted a hairless grizzly of a rubby, a chain cigar chewer.

"Don't let in nobodies!" He barreled out of the tub with no underwear, big El Dorado in his chaw.

"Dee guy next door dere, Jean-Jean, he's very bad man. He's take my Timex. He's take my ring. He's take my télévishun. You watch out. He's takes dope. He's come and he's fix me in my bed like dis."

He clamped his wet hands around my throat.

"Next munt, I go live wid my mudderr."

I thanked him for the tip, then closed the door as he toweled his genitals stark naked in the corridor.

I never had the pain of meeting Jean-Jean. But I did catch a glimpse of the cross he bore from his left ear lobe. The jewel glowed in the dark of a police cruiser, brighter than the badge of the cop to whom he was handcuffed.

Once there was a brawl — I thought. "Ben crime!" and "tabernacks," rattled the stairway. It was Montréal muscle hauling up a pew they had ripped off from a church of their choice.

"Wolfman" (I'm sure his mother called him Bébé), shouldered the most spectacular head of hair I have ever beheld on an uncaged human. The split ends rapunzeled past his calves.

"I 'ave a hundred-dollar-a-day shampoo habit!" He would growl every time I interrupted him in the bathroom.

He never fastened his red shock of hair into a ponytail. But you could always hear him howling around the toilet, long long locks stuffed inside his back pockets. Talk about furfur.

I lost count of the Jeans and Jacques. Most of them looked like kissing cousins of Paul Rose: agonized faces in army surplus fatigues worn throughout winter, sans scarves or gloves. LaBelle Bar-B-Q *habitués*. They smoked *La Québécoise* coffin nails when no "mari" was adrift in the province, were Pink Floyd buffs, and apolitical *Péquistes*.

Only one spooked me: Pierre. Taller than Mr. Muffler, a pockmarked goalie mask of a complexion, four Canadian silver dollars plugged as buttons to his bomber jacket, two rhinestone-studded wristbands, bigfoot combat boots, a fleury crucifix around his neck tinkling with a coke spoon, he shot me his straightest smile while requesting ten bucks. How do you say no to all that artillery? I padded over to my bookcase and extracted a Peking edition of Mao Tse-Tung's little red book. The flyleaf was lined with emergency money. Two blue Wilfred Lauriers equal one purple Sir John A. MacDonald certifies the mint in Ottawa. So I surrendered two blue Lauriers. That settled that account. I spotted Pierre next on the front page of Photo Police, reposed in a casket.

And only one charmed me: Chantal. I bumped into her hanging up her wash in brrrrrr November weather. She was wearing nothing but a brassiere, slacks, slippers, and a wedding ring. Wooden clothes pegs were clipped about her bra cups. We nodded *bonjour*. I twist-tied the weekend's waste into a Glad bag and went inside. As if epiphanies didn't happen in Québec anymore!

The occupancy rate was desperado rapid in that funhouse. I asked the landlord to install turnstiles instead of doors. Crashers and dashers did one night stands. Even sleep had to be stolen. But I had never popped eyes on that girlie-next-door before. And she was obviously very much at home!

That evening there was a love tap on my door. It was her. Could she borrow a dollar for cigarettes please? *Mon plaisir.* She complimented me on how spic and span my kitchenette was "for a man." And so many books! In the cupboard, in the sink, on the floor. And was that my guitar she could hear through the walls? Or a record?

I apologized for the racket. I was a practicing musician. Could she have a try? *Mon plaisir.* She grabbed my Martin and swung into a sweet Laura-C-chord song. She smiled better than she sang. She forgot the lyrics. Discouraged by her miscue, the instrument landed back on my lap. Her husband frowned upon women with guitars, something lesbian about it. Women of learning do not study guitar. He was a man of training, a *programmeur analyste*.

"He speak t'ree language, my husband: English, French, and Cobol!"

They were temporarily separated. She was cooped up in this hole-in-the-wall-roof-and-floor until marital differences could be patched up. Reconciliation was as impossible as making two islands meet. He originated from Ile Jésus, she from St. Henri.

She invited me over to her room.

"Don't be shy. I don't eat you."

"Next time."

The following evening: same rap of love taps. Could she use my phone please? *Mon plaisir.* Next morning: could she borrow some toothpaste? *Mon plaisir.* Next: a book? *Mon plaisir.* Next: S.O.S. scouring pads? *Mon plaisir.* Her husband entered our conversation as often as she entered my bachelor's paradise. Male intuition warned me that she was seeking a peg for her hangups. Don't get involved.

Despite the clockwork knocks, she was a delight to listen to. Her *Canayen français* "switch reflex" answered you in English, even if you addressed her in French. She was pretty when she didn't try to be pretty, bouffant perm bleached white as angel hair, figure like a diet Pepsi bottle full of that sexy avoirdupois, the woman in western *chez-nous* hurtin' songs. Chantal startled me when she admitted she was only 20, married three years, no kids. She looked 30, and troubled.

Then just as I predicted, there was a fire. An overdecorated Christmas tree on the bottom floor flared up like the burning bush. Because of the stench from the oil heater, I didn't smell a whiff. A commotion shook the foundation — but that was normal. When a firetruck pulled up, and I spotted black cumulus billowing out under my window, I knew it wasn't Wolfman roasting chestnuts.

I ran out kissing Miss Martin and Miss Gibson: my two guitars. Less valuable possessions were stashed inside unopened boxes — a contingency plan for such *prestissimo* get-aways. Naturally, the night was Arctic cold. A fireman welcomed us to warm our toes inside the truck. But what could beat the heat of your own home and hearth going up in smoke? No flames, only black malodorous fumes, thick enough to smut the snow, wafted out of bashed-in glass.

Bugs Benny, a doper and unemployed welder, clacked his heels back and forth to stay warm. His gum-chewing girlfriend hugged an orange Angora cat to her chest. The pussy was called Sunkist. We huddled in a circle with two other tenants harmonizing "Light My Fire."

"You think yuz got it tough." A bystander grumbled. "Why our's burned down smack down ta the slab whilst my ol' man was lyin' dead in a funeral parlor. Mortgage paid 'n' all. Smack down ta the slab. Hell, this ain't nothin' compared ta our's. This is jist a housewarmin' compared ta our's...."

The wet blanket wanted sympathy from us! Sense of humor, give me strength. Where would I sleep in the ashes? Would I have to move again? Did I leave anything behind? Was anyone still up there?

Chantal was missing. Prior to the outbreak, she had quarreled with her spouse on my telephone. She had gussied herself up like a female impersonator. I couldn't help impressions. She really revved up the Revlon for him, even for a mere chat on the phone. But no one had noticed her departure.

I wooshed up the staircase to make sure. The air inside was breathable, but smarts on the eyes. There she lay, in bed, empty bottle of Mandrax beside her overdosed head.

"Chantal! Chantal!" I yelled into her ear.

"Wake up! Wake up! There's a fire! *Feu! Feu!*"

My hands were too numb to feel her forehead or pulse. I allez-ooped her up into my arms. Chivalry was not dead, and neither was she. Chantal moaned to be released, so I laid her down again. But the sleeping beauty wouldn't budge. I whacked her across a cheekbone hard enough to see red crosses. She lazied over and sat up, headache in her hands, mumbling something like "allez, allez" or "Alain, Alain" — her husband's name.

I rushed her a glass of water. She smashed it to the ground. Nausea from smoke inhalation began to tug at my guts. I felt like vomiting. Chantal was too hot to handle. So I charged out, right into the platoon chief. He was marching up the stairs to inspect our landing, finally.

They had to forcibly remove Chantal. She honestly wanted to die. A crowd of spectators had poofed out of the cracks. We eyewitnessed, as Chantal kicked and bucked in back of an MUC ambulance. She screamed louder than the siren. Two constables and a para-medic sat on her. Painted lady. At least the fire was under control. A one alarmer. The eruption left no persons homeless. We already were.

The noise of the ambulance jammed out the piped-in carols on the street. Two red revolving lights from two police cruisers slashed at the night. Standing room only, I stared from the sidewalk, choked up, for the wrong reasons.

Next week, I was the one rapping love taps

on Chantal's door. She wasn't back. Then one evening, I chanced upon the runaway wife coming in with her groceries. She appeared to have recovered. Her stomach had been pumped with Silastic tubes, and her brain with psychiatric tests. I disclosed to her that our landlord had been summoned for investigation. Only the first floor had suffered severe damage. The upper two levels smelled worse than a million DuMauriers.

"Too bad I like menthol." She grinned, her old self again.

I extended a guilt-edged invitation to get together sometime. Would she remember her earlier entreaties? Would it still matter?

"Don't be shy," I mimicked her. "I don't eat you."

"Okee. We 'ave big pizza tonight. In my 'ouse. Okee?"

"Ooookeee!" I leaped down the stairs five steps at a time. I hurried to buy the best medicine in town, vodka, before the liquor commission closed.

Chantal made her own pizza with heaps of meat and cheese and mushrooms and aphrodisiac ingredients she had picked up at a health food store. Some fruitcake, which she had also baked, was left over from the holidays. I wished I could cook on a stove like her. She wished she could cook on a guitar like me! I played her "Strawberry Fields" for dessert. She said it was too depressing. So I tried "Tutti Frutti" — a fast Italian number. She didn't laugh, and insisted upon tidying up alone. She puffed on her menthols vexatiously. Sob stories seemed to cheer her up.

Chantal was the only child of two alcoholics. Her father had been a letter carrier. Her mother could hardly carry herself. Each Christmas they received charity baskets. One sad Noël, in a drunken fit, her father had dumped the donations down the old-fashioned snow chute on Ste. Ambroise street. The work crew chuckled as the food vanished under an avalanche of dirty snow. Chantal vowed never to live there again, to do everything in her powerlessness to be free.

She left home at the age of 16, landed a job at Rossy's, and enrolled in secretarial night school. The placement service found her an exciting, challenging, and rewarding career, as a scab. She was such an *ingénue*. During a white collar strike, she believed picket lines could be trespassed as safely as undefended borders. Thrashing her way through, a protester straightened her out by smearing her lipstick across her face. Thus trickled in Chantal's first nickels and dimes of independence.

She had met Alain while working at a Caisse-Populaire. He was a regular customer, and doll. It was a Minute Rice marriage. The love lasted one week — the length of their honeymoon in Acapulco. Chantal was born to be the helpmate of a truck driver. Her conduct showed it. Alain knew it. She would hide behind a chill smile and double daiquiri at parties. Chantal had overheard one of Alain's buddies, a fellow project co-ordinator, asking him if she had an I.Q. bigger than her shoe size? Both men tittered. Alain had only married her for her looks. Chantal knew it. Alain cared for stock-option plans and essential commodities, more than bonds of affection. Declines led advances during their first year together. Chantal lost interest in Alain's cynical Optimist Club *confrères*, porno videocassette swapping, or floating in the swimming pool like a rose inside a bowl behind their exurbia Brossard bungalow. Alain supplied her with luxury she did not demand, but for which she was grateful, at the expense of a love he could not provide. He desired a baby. She didn't. He desired a career for her. She didn't. Chantal had no ambition to be a mother, a career girl, or anything, but herself. All the incompatabilities she had assumed she could change in him, she couldn't. And vice versa.

Chantal got her rocks off on dancing. She could shake her tailfeathers all night at discotheques. Boogaloo in the loo! Clog to Magog! She adored jazz and classical ballet. But Alain's untrained eyes always fell asleep at Place des Arts during performances of *Les Grands Ballets Canadien*. The tutus toes-eed around the same way for what seemed like hours, he complained. The ballet he enjoyed most was composed of skates and bodychecks on Forum ice.

After the couple split, Chantal was left on the lawn, literally. No quality home to call home, no quality friend to call friend, Alain suggested his parents' duplex for accomodation. But that wasn't separation, that was sovereignty association!

Chantal nursed no fear of sharing the same lodgings with transients. Her curling iron snipped at the air. If any of those bastards came too close, she would "*zap leur zigou-zigou*" — electrocute their balls.

Chantal de-polydented her dentures and commenced brushing them. It was time to say goodbye. Her toothless gums invited me back again.

"Don't be shy. I don't eat you."

We laughed. Then I kissed her thank you on the cheek, same side where I had slapped her during the ordeal. I think she realized it too, and stroked mine, fondly.

One airless nightfall, I opened my battered door to the elements. Chantal popped in with a peekaboo. Her eyes glowed with such joy you could almost harness them for energy. She was hiding something behind her back. It was a present. For me. A book. One of those self-improvement guides that keep getting worse.

So we rendezvoused to her apartment — for self-improvement. Miss Martin accompanied us, plus a heeltap of vodka. Chantal chained her door so the "voyous" around us couldn't eavesdrop. But that only encouraged their Peeping Tomfoolery. Chantal chased them away, cursing like a witch. She then returned to her room with the dignity of a chatelaine. Nevertheless, the bums could still be heard through the woodwork, belching and farting and sneezing as loud as air brakes.

Master of unceremoniousness, I pledged a toast to the success of our survival in this firetrap. I let go a whoop while all the beer inside of Chantal burst into song. She rested her head on my shoulder as we made up rhymes.

Mon pays ce n'est pas un pays,
C'est la télé!
Mon jardin ce n'est pas un jardin,
C'est Complexe Desjardins!

Or a tune for atonal glass clinkers:

You hit sharp,
I hit flat,
Together we play *plat plat Plattsburgh!*

Coins and applause caromed off the exterior walls, shaking the plaster loose, acclaiming us as the official house band.

We took a breather. Chantal kept slamming a decrepit Zenith television until it came on. She didn't like the English channels. Murky resolution. She settled for a lurid foreign film overdubbed in French. The slow European pacing was *blasé* compared to our contrast, volume, and color. I had acquitted myself with such blistering virtuosity that my fingers were developing trumpeter's lip. She didn't have any chairs. So we curled up on her bed, sharing the last Molson.

"*Voyons! Nous sommes maître chez nous!*" I raised the bottle.

"Oooo! *Gardes! Gardes!*" Chantal covered her eyes.

Count Dracula's Gothic château invaded our 1-room castle. We wondered where those monsters had learned to play organ so well? Probably from Hollywood mounties. Before you could whisper Lon Chaney Junior have a heart, I fell asleep, dead tired.

Chantal roused me awake. She had boiled some coffee. I faded away again. So she shut the TV, and opened herself up. An album of photographs plopped on my lap.

"You stay," she implored with a moue.

"I stay." Slurp.

Preserved between creased pages were images from childhood: her hair plain brown, cropped short like a nun's; a formal shot of her First Communion (first vows to lose value), bareheaded belle kneeling on a prie-dieu without the veil she had singed accidentally clutching her candle too close, lily of the valley on her lace, cavities in her teeth; a group shot of her singing hosanna for the Ste. Cunégonde girls glee club; snapshots of pets, her mother's birthday party, her father's funeral. Instamatic lifetimes.

My eyes became filmy with sleep. Chantal's hazel irises gleamed as bright as a night owl's. She filled a saucer with Hostess potato chips.

"*Tiens.* You stay."

"I stay." Chomp.

Out slid slides of her wedding: cutting the cake, signing the register, spoony kiss with Alain on the right, spoony kiss with Alain on the left. Quite a flashing blade.

Then she extracted a cartoon of *Le Professeur Pi.* His stenographer had just crowned him on the noggin with a typewriter. He was a "*gross jambon*" — a stuffed shirt, like her ex-boss.

A 3 x 5 of a man holding a dead swan aloft came next. He was a distant uncle in Alberta. He had bagged the Whistler illegally.

"*Y'sont bêtes, les hommes. Bêtes! Bêtes!*" She pouted at the dead swan.

Her pout spread into a proud smile. She unfolded a clipping, a close-up of herself in the *Sourire de matin* section of *Montréal matin*, her Rossy days. It was the smile of a cheerleader on the losing side: hazel eyes a hazy shade of merry, dimple alone suitable for framing. She was so simple, so fetching. I saw why Alain had grabbed her so fast. I was touched.

I was also very, very, groggy. Chantal used her feminine wiles to pass away more wee minutes.

"I 'ave lots I can show you." She undid the drawstring to her nightie.

Stretching out on the bed, nonchalantly, she urged me to examine her pelvis. There was something on it. A scar.

"See. Dat's where I kill myself."

The wound was almost invisible without a magnifying glass. The cut had been inflicted with a pen knife. It couldn't have spurted more than a thimbleful of blood, a job for Curad ouchless. My finger journeyed across the white cicatrice, no wider than a fingerbreadth. You didn't have to be a surgeon to see the pain was in her heart.

Chantal's flesh felt so luscious. My one-finger massage multiplied into five. I could spy the areola of one nipple rising toward me. I could also spy her curling iron. Her eyes were warm. Consenting? Why did she buy me that present? Naw. The book wasn't pornography. But why the *entre-nous*? Overtures? Naw. I radiated more Red Shield appeal than sex appeal. But would she think me too forward if I did? Or too backward if I didn't? Her cleavage beckoned for visitors more mysteriously than Ausable Chasm. *Don't be shy, I don't eat you.* Naw. Alain was more visible in her mind than I was, or else why reveal his scars? I felt like a prick and removed myself off her bedsheets.

Now I couldn't go to sleep! Was she looking for nookie just a 20-carat wedding ring's throw away? Or was she just very lonely? The hoarfrost on my windowpane created a *trompe l'oeil* design as on a Playtex bra. Naw. It was all a mistake. Fantasy follies. Chantal would have had the decency to wear her dentures.

It was a good thing I did a "*tirez*" and pulled out, instead of a "*poussez*" and push my luck. Chantal had come a long way from Hail Marys to Bloody Marys, but not that far. The next day, after her customary love taps on my door, she introduced me to Alain. The pair were off to the hospital, a joint appointment with her analyst. I ushered them into my "office." *Non merci.* Time was pressing. Sporting a maxicoat, Foster Grant shades, and Montréal's finest moustache, Alain came across as personable but untalkative; a gold-credit-card-carrying member of the *entrepreneuriat*. My books bemused him: high culture, low income.

What had occurred the night before had very definitely not been seduction. I was a pleasant victim of Chantal's hospitality, her angel-may-care attitude toward living.

January palled into February, February into March. The rheumatic reindeer days of winter dragged on. Everything and everyone operated at a stationary low — everyone except Chantal and I. Our impermanent relationship heightened. We shopped together, went bowling, ate hot dogs and fries at Woolworth, devoured the latest disaster flick. She covered up at the sight of blood; I covered up at the sight of breasts. Her elbow would nudge me to behave.

Outdoors, in minus-Celsius sunlight, Christmas decorations were already being stripped down. Red papier-mâché bells that didn't ring, burned-out lightbulbs for clappers, sooty sparklers in traffic light colors: the spirit of jubilation snuffed out by the dreary humbug of winter.

Chantal and I guarded the spirit. She slithered her arm under mine and squeezed me to her tight.

"Jingo bells! Jingo bells! Jingo all le way!"

"Ho-ho-ho! Ho Chi Minh! Yamaha-ha-ha! Hey!" I huffed and puffed to see who could blow the biggest vapor clouds.

Dining made speaking easier. So we frequented the choicest local restaurants and brasseries. Her conversation always centered around Alain's shortcomings. She was commuting to Brossard once a week, frightened to go back. If the marriage failed again, that was it. *Fini*, flop.

But her *joual* would giddyup into supertest horsepower and flash back and forth over how war brides of yore looked like grannies and tear-jerkers make her giggle and no true *Montréalais* ever rides a *calèche* except during transit strikes and why do extra-terrestials in movies always speak with Oxford accents and *colline de bines* last call already!

April came. Winter ended abruptly. So did Chantal's unemployment insurance. She was clearing out. She was tired of living with people "raised by wolves." We threw a homecoming party. Just the two of us were invited. Chantal had purchased a Genesis exercise computer for Alain. The gizmo strapped to the wrist like a watch and recorded your pulse rate while jogging. I wanted to give it a trial run on the spot. But Chantal insisted that I was too skinny, "micro thin," and had to concentrate on gaining weight. So she stuffed me with meat pie and potato salad and cheese and a brick of ice cream. To unstiffen, we went for a stroll along the boardwalk.

The river was as polluted as ever, dishwater gray, too ugly for a postcard but still beautiful to me. Chantal missed it too. We skimmed pebbles across whirlpools. The waterfront was the spitting image of a tundra, three-and-a-half kilometres of barren landfill, a reclamation project. A woodlot lay crushed beneath shitty scheiste for a new mantle of civic green.

Chantal hopscotched upon caterpillar tractor marks — her *petite ballet Canadienne* for the fish and I. She danced *jêtes* and *tendus* over mud puddles, a pirouette on a plank of wood. We strutted a tango together, cheek to cheek, to the river's edge, jiggling our jollies each time we nearly tipped over into the dropoff. I muffed an *entrechat* and landed on my royal *derrière*.

"Wo! You dance like a 'orse!" She whipped my behind.

"You mean like a robot."

"Rowbutt? What is dat? Rowbutt?"

I explained. Of course, Chantal had to whir and click and beep, blinking eyes ON and OFF, flipping false teeth in and out.

I dusted myself off, then sat on a boulder, relaxing, keeping the rock warm for her. She nestled beside me. Things became thud quiet.

We watched, and watched the river. Though headwinds were heavy, the center appeared at a standstill. Freshets surged toward gulfs. There were no birds. Spring tides brought a natural high. The boardwalk owed its existence to floods a century ago when this place was a dumping ground for Fenians, gaolbirds, blackamoors, dollymops, dagos, foreigners and other non-talkers. I picked myself up and stirred the icy meltwater. A bare hand couldn't linger longer than a second. The river made me shiver. When the sense of the St. Lawrence had dispersed, I gazed up at Chantal. Her eyes were flooded, with tears.

By twist of fate, I was out in back hogtying another Glad bag, when Chantal knocked to say goodbye. They must have been love taps, because I didn't hear. The engine of Alain's BMW generated such a fanfare that I glanced out the window. Chantal was stepping into the car. She closed the door, checked her hair and make-up in the rear-view mirror, and never looked back.

But our paths did crisscross one more time. We bumped into each other under the direction arrows amid islands of merchandise at Pascal's hardware. It was midsummer, one year later, though it seemed ice ages ago since we had been foul-weather friends. She was very gracious, and very pregnant.

"If it's a boy, call it Wolfman. Okay?"

She wasn't amused. No more *bonhomie*? We sortied into a parking lot where she showed off her brand new station wagon, a Chrysler LeBaron: power windows, power steering, power brakes. It was her car. She waddled about the four doors with the aloofness of a model in a commercial.

I just wanted to look at her: nails still bitten, hair still bouffant dyed a frostier silver, eyes still hazel and hazy. She was changing into the wife of *Professeur Pi*. Yet her features retained a dark, drawn, aspect; the opposite of her abdomen. Such a condition was not unusual during a period of expectancy. Only her gynecologist knew for sure — and her analyst.

"*Tu es contente.*" I asked declaratively.

"*Oui, tiens*, touch."

She pressed my palm to her belly. I felt nothing, embarrassed. It was like touching a part of Alain, a very private part.

"He keeps a good beat," I improvised. "He'll be a good drummer."

We exchanged two-handed handshakes, bidding adieu properly. She didn't mention saying hi again at some future date. The situation wasn't exactly inviting.

But as she drove off in her station wagon, I could still hear her screaming in the back of an ambulance, crying for death. Now a fetus in her womb was kicking for dear life. *Chère Chantal*, with her love of everyone's music but her own; and her squeamish fear of blood, but her own. I thought of the suicide scar, and hoped, in a small way, the birth would not be caesarean.

The Best Ice in Quebec

Debussy to Beau Dommage, Mrs. Murray bought them all, for her house plants. Music brought out the euphoria in flora. African violets grew more animated with Irish ballads. Cactus loved Kiss. Lavenders leaned toward Handel's "Water Music." And Wandering Jews enjoyed a good hum.

Mrs. Murray's son had introduced her to the Light Classics. He was a jade businessman in British Columbia. His son had initiated her into Heavy Metal rock. He was a self-absorbed beach-comber. But horticulture was all Mrs. Murray cared for. During the Depression, she had converted a sunless dirt yard into a vegetable patch. Heart-shaped tomatoes had ripened as large as her own heart. Neighbors in her "Point St. Charles plantation" would pilfer her good earth for their window boxes.

Now it was the spring of 1977. The first separatist government in the history of Québec had been elected that fall. And there was talk of a greater Depression on English and French tongues. I had rented the apartment out of which Mrs. Murray had just moved; not to cross provincial borders, but across the street.

Despite the wishful thinking of local francophones, Lafleur Street was not named after Guy Lafleur, The Flying Frenchmen's right winger; but after a dull alderman, as usual. The side street was a "dead neck" which doglegged toward the waterfront. The road had been built for horses and buggies, not V-8 Pintos and Mustangs. One more crack in the surface and you could declare an earthquake. Swings and seesaws in Therien Park tottered between clotheslined back yards and the St. Lawrence. The dampness from the river made my bunker smell like a shoe. The building itself slanted from shrinkage and wear. I imagined the huge decaying structure as a kind of three-storey tombstone for dead sparrows I discovered under the porch, or in potholes. The red bricks had blackened, along with a cement maple leaf embossed on the façade. No other leaves in sight.

The inhabitants were mostly English-speaking pensioners. They treated the tenement as a self-run nursing home, sharing meals, clothes, furniture, and medicine like second childhood toys. Some had known each other since their first childhood, never setting down roots in any other city. The atmosphere exuded a died-in, rather than a lived-in quality. Mrs. Murray sold me a fridge which belonged to her friend Ron in no. 3. He was dead. She sold me a heater which belonged to her friend June in no. 8. She was dead. She sold me a bed which belonged to her friend Gus in no. 9. He died in it.

I was still receiving her mail after half a year. Instead of entrusting the two envelopes to our absent-minded janitor (the tenants took care of him), I decided to deliver them myself. There was no better excuse to hear more of her stories. I loved the way the lore just spun out of her like yarn off an old-fashioned niddy noddy.

Her new lodgings were situated within a leaning row of brick houses. "Dominoes," she called them. You could almost hear the lime-based mortar joints creaking for a repointing job. A cement cinquefoil adorned her front. Beavers served as mason marks on others. Wildlife, which had once breathed here, were now captured in the tracery. How deep were the Iroquois bones under the pavement? The way of weak minorities.

I rang the doorbell, glancing through her window into a forest of hanging baskets.

"Special delivery!"

"Oh hullo, c'mon in!"

A portrait of Our Lady of Perpetual Help gave me the once-over as I removed my jacket. The interior smelled like a greenhouse. Mrs. Murray escorted me on a tour of her new premises. Her son had come over from Victoria to install the cushion floors, a new draft for the furnace, a doorbell, a modern toilet box, as well as to paint the bedroom and kitchen, repair the spalling along the window lintels, and to erect a partition on the back gallery. The "kinky kids" next door had frazzled her clothesline with a crowbar. One morning, she awoke to the sight of a rubber dildo planted in one of her outdoor pots.

Her four rooms had been used as a crash pad and marijuana den by some "burn-baby-burn bums."

"I was scrapin' the smoke offa them ceilings like mud!"

Now you could eat off her floors. Everything was in its place — including me in a recliner, cup of tea in my hands, spoon on the right, sugar cube on the left, warm feeling inside. Greenery was positioned as strategically near light and shade as scatter rugs near feet going in or out. Fuchsia, Hibiscus, Rosemary, and Oleander were shelved on a regency style mahogany whatnot. A yesterday-today-and-tomorrow plant decorated her antique drop-leaf table. She offered me home-baked chocolate chip cookies from a biscuit barrel with a wicker handle and hand- painted meadow larks. Roses in her arms, St. Teresa of Avila watched over ferns and palms beside a Waterbury steeple clock. Pope John XXIII eyed the roses reverently. Photographs of next-of-kin hung beside saints. And beside them, thrived more kingdoms of flowers.

"So this is where all the flowers have gone?"

She wrinkled her brow, puzzled.

"I mean the trees and flowers that once bloomed on the street here."

"Oh them, yes. Once the river was so fresh and pure you could sip the water with a straw. Now you don't know what's comin' out the tap? Molson's Canadian."

They say humans who live alone with pets acquire the characteristics of their animals after a while, and vice versa. By some heliotropic miracle, Mrs. Murray took after her perennials: colorful and whimsical with no rejuvenation necessary. Plump as a blimp, shaky as a winding staircase, her age only showed when she walked. Her sense of balance had obviously been tempered by unsteady supports.

"Have yuh seen all the houses for sale in the Gazette lately?" She asked in a concerned tone of voice. "Everybody's leavin'. Pretty soon the whole paper's gonna be one big want-ad for real estate from front to back. A book of Exodus."

"Well, René Lévesque hasn't knocked on my door yet in the middle of the night."

"I feels the same way, love. Been livin' here near eighty years and my guardian angels has always seen me through."

She lifted up her eyes toward the roof, as if a squadron of dominions, principalities, and cherubim were on patrol up there.

"Mind, if worse comes to worse, I can high-tail it to my son's in B.C. I practically had to summon the chariot of the gods just to move my worldly goods across the curb! Used to be I could fly with the owls all night and keep up with the eagles all day. Now I just sits and waits for my hockey to come on. Oh yes, I miss that Fergy! You remember John Ferguson? *Fou-fou* number 22!''

''Yeah. Mr. Sin Bin.''

''Oh, he was made a scrap iron that one. And there was the Gumper. Humpty Dumpty we used to call him on Burgess street when he was just a wee little boy. And Bobby Hull don't bless himself no more before steppin' on the ice.''

''Well, he's lost all his teeth and made all his money.''

''Well it ain't hockey no more with expansion and all that. Now it's just hokey. Huh, huh.''

''You must be used to it by now, Mrs. Murray. You're older than the NHL!''

''But still too young for lawn bowlin'! Well, I still takes the grandkids when they comes over for the holidays to see the Verdun Maple Leafs at the Auditorium.''

''Oh yeah, I haven't been there since my rink rat days. I used to skip school just to watch the Montreal Canadiens put on their skates. You could peek through a grating on the dressing room window. And if you stood outside the front door, Dickie Moore or Jean Beliveau or Boom Boom Geoffrion would give you spending money, or signed pictures of themselves. I snuck in once and nobody said anything. They probably thought I was the owner's son. Henri Richard gave me his stick. Too bad there wasn't much of a blade on it, about as long as his autograph. The Canadiens still practice there. I remember Doug Harvey telling Toe Blake that it's the best ice in Quebec.''

''Well love, we was playin' the sport out in the fields when it was still called 'shinny,' eh? We'd collect all the horsebuns that was frozen on the street and use 'em for pucks. There was piles and piles in the old dump on Libre street where the horses lugged the garbage. We used umbrella handles for sticks, or any ol' plywood lying around. My brother was always in goal. He'd put on puttees my dad had from the war. Stuff 'em with newspapers cause they wouldn't fit. But we'd end up shootin' at each other no matter what side we was on for the fun of smashin' them horsebuns on our behinds. There was this French lad once who wanted a game with us. Could take us all on by himself, he said. He had this retarded brother he was minding who used to follow him around like a shadow. The poor little shaver was too feeble to play, so he'd just sit in a snowbank and clap whenever someone got hit. Strike one! Strike one! That was all he could blather like a baseball ump. They came from a big family, the size of a hockey team. You know how the French Catholics had the do-re-mi for makin' babies, eh? Basketcases under every bed. Sisters sleepin' with brothers to continue the race. So anyways, there was five of us against one-and-a-half of him. And he just got pasted and pasted that poor lad. But he was a hellfighter. Oh my goodness, he'd stomp and he'd rave crazier than a canal horse. We asked him if he wanted to change sides? But no, he just kept on a-playin' with tears in his eyes. So we kept on pastin' and pastin' him. He even got a bloody nose. When we ran out of horsebuns, we used his brother's glove as a puck until it got dark. Then we went in and we never saw him again. They got heart the French. They got heart."

Rain spindrifted upon her windowpane. A silver thaw was rehearsing for a downpour. Her eyes gazed serenely at the leaden clouds in motion. Bits of vapor fogged visibility. The winter-stained glass served as a DEW line between herself and the outside world. Stare long enough, go stir crazy.

"Looks like it's going to rain." I sipped my tea.

"Just a devil's wet dream, my husband used to say. Might have to miss my French course tonight."

"You're taking French?"

"*Oui monsieur*, I'm takin' French! It's about time this here colleen, I was sayin' to myself, finally learned what them peppers have been whippin their lips about all these years! But it's hard, yuh know. They talk so fast, like Telex machines. And all they talk about is sex. Some people will tell ya my English is all screwball. But it's gettin' so bad here in the providence of Quebec that we're bein' buried alive. Buried alive under all them newfangled legislations.''

''The French felt the same way for two hundred years.''

''Lookit. I went down this winter to the Verdun General for this abscess in my ear, see. Headaches and earaches non-stop I've had from it. When the guck bursts, I can feel it goin' down my throat. Just awful. So nine o'clock sharp, I'm the first one there, right? You know what happened? 6:30 comes around, and I'm still there, the last to leave. They saw my name was Anglo-Saxon. And when I gets in the office, the doctor talks to me in French. I says to him I don't speak French. He says what are you doing here? I says my ear is sick. He says show me your card. I shows him my card. He says it's old and I need a new one. I says pretty soon I'll need a new ear! So the nurse makes out this new card, all in French. Come back in two months, *s'il vous plait*. I says I can't sleep from the pain. She says buy a thermos bottle. So I comes back in two months. He gets an electric drill, sticks it in my ear, takes out the guck, in two seconds it's over. I'm not goin' there again.''

''The French lessons will cure that.''

''Well don't ask me to say nothin' yet, eh? The teacher's from France. He tells us jokes. You know what PQ stands for? 'Pack quick'!''

''What else have you learned, Mrs. Murray?''

''Well, I'z been listenin' to my hockey in French, eh? But it's not as excitin'. Sounds like a chess game the way they announce it. You only hear cheers when it's over. Our teacher tells us we should phone in those hot line shows to express our opinions in French. He says the whole country should be a classroom. But I dunno. I'm so scared to go out now. I was comin' home the other night from my courses, con-conjure-conjurgratin' them future perfects in my head, when you know what happens? This buncha trash on two legs, I swear they weren't a minute over ten years old, starts tearin' and a-tuggin' at my purse. So I just pushes 'em aside and tells 'em to go do their homework. You think they'd listen? No sir. The smart-alecs start kickin' at my ankles and pullin' and a-yankin' at my purse again. So lord have mercy, I just hauls off and hits 'em with my hardest haymaker. You think that scares them no-good-single-mother's sons? Nosiree. My heart almost stops when I see one of them pick up this chunk of ice. Then the other rolls a snowball and throws it at my bad back. The ice hits me in the face and knocks me over like a ten pin. So I starts screamin' and a-yellin' blue murder, eh? And the little buggers start yellin' back '*maudite nana! maudite nana!*'. So I yells back 'I'll *maudite nana* you!' I goes home and calls the police. They asks me if I can identify the little terrorists? But they all looks the same with their snotty faces and dirty fingernails. I tell yuh, love. I raised my young ones during the Dirty Thirties — though I don't know why they called 'em that.

They were clean times compared to now. And we had no welfare, eh? My husband, God rest his soul, used to say he'd rather be a dead stiff in a coffin than a pogey stiff on a porch. A beautiful man he was. But tougher than bully beef if anyone ever crossed him. A beautiful marriage we had, fifty six years. We never had much frippery to show off. But we didn't need much. An atomic bomb couldn't split us apart. He built that Auditorium you know? It was a relief project for the unemployed then. Prouder 'n tavern preachers, he and I, we'd go to rasslin' matches or carnivals inside that building. Like it was in our own house. But the last time I took the grandkids, I got such a chill. You couldn't talk to the guy beside ya. All the hockey players were French. And we got blitzed by so many chip bags, it was like an air raid in the last doo! It's almost as if they were aimin' at yuh cuz you're English."

"Now that's paranoia, Mrs. Murray. You've been reading too many scareheads."

"My head ain't scared."

"In other countries it would have been bullets instead of snowballs."

Frozen between her fixed income and her feudal faith, my cold comfort must have been an icicle on a platter for her. She made no effort to respond. I made no effort to continue. I had come to deliver her letters, not my epistle.

"Do you have French friends who could help you with your studies?"

"Well, I worked with 'em for seventeen years, eh? My girlfriend and I, makin' silhouettes in the sewing room at DIL, before they condemned it. She's French, and no separatist, let me tell yuh! Her husband is buried out in the Field of Honor in Pointe Claire. He put the Huns on the run with that regiment there that sounds like waterfalls—Chaudyears?"

"*Chaudières*," I corrected her.

"Well that's one thing they never think about when they cry '*Vive le Quebec libber!*' Not too many would die for this place. It's all a song to them. They'd have their submarine sandwich navy out there on Beaver Lake and that's it. My girlfriend and I go to the same church together. Notre Dame des Sept Dollars."

"It's *sept douleurs*, Mrs. Murray." I tried not to laugh. "Seven sorrows, not seven dollars!"

"Oh, it's all the same to them."

"Not to the language police."

"Listen, love, this flapdoodle about tongues; these French and English high rollers with their kewpie wives and their fancy property, I've polished their silverware and done their laundry, and I'm not impressed. They're not happy people. They just want things. I'll never be a martyr for *things*, huh huh. Fightin' and a-killin' each other for things. That's stupid. The robber barons up on the hill, or the thieves down here: the evil is equal. I've known true love in my life. If only this old head of mine had younger shoulders, I'd tell 'em all. Class is somethin' you carry inside of you, it has nothin' to do with money."

Our conversation had mushroomed into something more vast than the both of us. The political climate was affecting every living thing — except flowers. I examined a porcelain planter with a homestead scene on it.

"Well. At least it's quiet here."

"Oh! Wait 'til them Heinz 57's start meowlin' and howlin'! Now you know what a nice pet is? A parakeet. We had one for twenty two years on Favard street. The nuns had their farms all along it. You'd go to their door, they'd give ya turnip tops, you'd give 'em a quarter. Oh my my! How that bird loved turnip tops! You could take him outside and he wouldn't fly away. Every Wednesday, we'd ring-dang-tootle, the whole squawking brood of us, down to the bandstand they had near Hogan's bath. And that creature would try and sing along with us, even though he weren't no songbird. But he could tell how good we felt. And he'd flip off one shoulder and onto another and let strangers touch him and oh it was so lovely. But my sons would go fishin', eh? Over by Torchy Wharf. They'd bring back pike and perch and dore and catfish and shave 'em in the kitchen — where the bird cage was. Well my son Stephen, who died in the war, got the bright idea to cut out the eyes and train that clown of a bird to catch 'em in its beak. Well, my stars! When I saw that I said to them, if I catch yuh feedin' fisheyes to that parakeet one more time I'm gonna feed yuz the same thing the same way and seez how you like it!"

I put aside my cup and saucer. It was time to go.

"More tea, love? Somethin' to eat?"

"Mrs. Murray, you're a heavenly hostess."

Oak molding in the hallway was adorned with tea, toffee, and tobacco tins from England. One Rowntree collectible bore the profiles of George V and Queen Mary surrounded by scenes of Empire. A bisque statuette of St. Patrick on a cloverleaf base stood beside a lily atop a walnut trestle. The leaves drooped like spinach.

"This one's giving up the ghost."

"Oh, when they go limp on me I just plays 'em 'God Save the Queen.' That always straightens 'em to attention! Music and manure is all they need to survive. And there's plenty of both around here!"

"Well, don't play too loud now. The neighbors might get the wrong impression."

"Oh no, not me! Everythin's so loud nowadays. The music is splittin' yer ears. The marriages is splittin'. The country is splittin'. Even the NHL has more divisions!"

"I gotta be splitting too, Mrs. Murray. Thanks for everything. My hollyhocks say hi."

"Don't forget to tell me the little newses."

I hated to leave her. She was lonely for company. Her home smelled like a flower boutique, and not a hospital pharmacy as with some senior citizens.

I'll never forget how her golden aging fingers ran slowly along the edges of a hose-in-hose hybrid by the doorway.

"They're so lovely." She smiled. "I read to them in French yuh know, when I'm doin' my homework. They don't mind what language you talk. They're so lovely, so lovely. It's people who spoil everything."

WALKING ON CRIED RIVERS

"Please! Please! Please! Dr. Overbye! Please can I be Santa Claus this year? Can I? Can I? Can I?" Benny Hopper jounced up and down in his Harvey Wallbanger wheelchair. "I promise I won't paint any more dickey birds on those blue-and-white wheelchair signs! And I won't put any more magic mushrooms inside those Goodwill Sunday Suppers! And I won't blindfold Madame Chaudasse's Seeing Eye dog! Oh please! Please! Please! I'd go down on my knees if I had knees to go down on!"

"Who, or what was that?" the bandleader gawked in disbelief.

"Oh, that's Benny, one of our Code 9's," remarked Dr. Overbye, physician-in-chief and impresario behind this season's Christmas bash.

The two men trudged out of the general cold into the central heating of the Rehabilitation Institute.

"Code 9?"

"Yes. That's the term the courts use for patients with criminal tendencies. You know? The ones who swoop into your office waving Saturday night specials, or utility knives with six additional blades. All because they suspect you released them too early, or too late, or prescribed the wrong pills."

"You're kidding me."

"I wish I was. The lunatic fringe is developing into a bulge."

"For an amputee, he's got a lot of dash."

"Oh, Benny's no lambchop! He robs banks. He knows how to assemble bombs or false-bottom UNICEF cans. He fired a bullet through a box office window once because the management wouldn't let him in to see *The Rocky Horror Picture Show* without an aide. He's got one arm, and no legs, but he's rigged up a rescuphone transmitter to his wheelchair, an AM-FM radio, and a microcomputer. He's got a convertible toilet in there, a portable bar, and God knows what else? It's a cockpit. He's also a whiz at manipulating people. He's a pathological liar. He's been endowed with an encyclopedic brain. And he behaves like a big baby."

"You seem to have his track record memorized."

"Yes, well. He's given us the runaround often enough. He shrugs off any job we find him. His foster parents consider him an Achilles heel. And so he keeps being referred back to us."

A whirring object grazed off one of the bandleader's galoshes.

"Hey mister! You got a cleft hoof!"

It was Benny Hopper in his Harvey Wall-banger wheelchair: baby booties glued to the floorboard, baseball cards entwining the spokes.

"Please, Dr. Overbye. If I can't be Santa Claus, can my two remaining mortal fingers at least touchie-feelie this superstar's guitar?" Benny beseeched them. "Eh? Eh? Pretty please? He can prestidigitate his way through the challenging chord structures while I strum with my teeth. I believe in the rhythm method."

"You could use a crash course in driver education first!" The musician re-fastened his galoshes.

"Peace, brother! I am not of woman born. But I say peace unto you all. Tis the season of peace!" Benny crooked two peewee fingers in the air. "Ever hear of Django Rhinehart?"

"Oh yes, the gypsy ..."

"The gypsy! The GYPSY!!! The man is the patron saint of all guitar pickers! He only had two fingers just like me. But his inimitable virtuosity could make those strings sing faster than guitar freaks with five fingers! You know what I mean? I'm not talking about dainty flutes and lutes in the tea room. I'm talking about fiery, crepuscular, Club Saint-Germain *soul!*"

"Well, yes, I understand." The musician straightened himself out. "Django Rhinehart was quite a celebrity in Europe."

"Oh! I'm a celebrity too!" Benny twinkled. "I've been on all the major programs: Headstart, Outreach, AA, Methadone, Meals on Wheels."

"Don't get lost in orbit." The bandleader nursed his heel.

"Don't you dare ridicule me! I am not what you see! I am not a cripple! I do not feel like a creep! The global economy is crippled thanks to people like you! Nuclear reactors are crippled! Space age man is a spiritual cripple! The whole creepy entropic universe is crippled! What's your crutch, mister? The crucifix? The hammer? The sickle? The pen? The bottle? Sex? Drugs? Food? Sports? Travel? *Objets d'art?* Lotteries? Children? Pets? I'd rather be crippled on the outside than crippled inside like you!"

"Hey now! *Uno momento!* I wasn't laughing at..."

Before the guitarist could open his mouth, a hot gob of spit hit him.

"Next time it'll be blood!" Benny glowered.

"Benny! Buck up!" Dr. Overbye was enraged. "As an antidote for your logorrhea, how would you like to spend another silent night with your handler there keeping watch over you?"

A security guard grinned.

"Not Kierkegaard! Tell that fag to keep his helping hands off me! Or else he's going to get it right in the kisser!" Benny clenched his feisty two-fingered fist. "He's certainly no Gentleman Usher of the Black Rod! Come on, doc! Have mercy! Why can't I be Santa Claus on this feast that celebrates the birth of Christ? I never asked to be born. I'm just asking for this teeny weeny little consolation gift. Please? I'll feel like I'm walking on cried rivers."

Dr. Overbye raised a skeptical eyebrow. "I'll see what I can do."

He accompanied the bandleader into the reception hall.

"Oh! Doctor! Doctor!"

"Yes, Benny." Dr. Overbye pivoted.

"Can I at least carry the guitar case? I used to play for the Basement Bugaboo Blues Band and the Earwax Lickers. Retro stuff. We were discovered in a Brazilian jungle by a former Nazi war criminal with a vengeance."

Dr. Overbye looked at the musician. The musician looked at his guitar case, Benny Hopper looked at them both with one squinting eye.

"Well." The musician wavered. "Okay."

He eased his Gretsch across the arm rests of the wheelchair. The hardshell case barricaded Benny in. Only his scalp protruded, short and curly like pubic hair. His fingers tweezed the plastic handle. He transported the instrument into the hall with the whatever-gets-you-through-the-night fidelity of a roadie.

''Thank you.'' The musician shook Benny's clawhammer of a hand.

''You play deadbeat music.'' Benny noticed a drum machine on the stage.

''Benny, aren't you going to say thank you too?'' Dr. Overbye hinted.

''No! I should charge him a freight rate! This guy was too cheap to even let me try his guitar!''

''That's not very thoughtful of you.''

''Oh, I'm surrounded by thoughtful people. I'm sorry. I can't think at room temperature. I'm a seedless cucumber. I never learned how to say thank you.''

''Well now's a good time to start.''

''Oh, sheeesh! What kind of a turkey do you think I am?'' Benny waved ta-ta. ''This is Christmas, not Thanksgiving!''

Benny whirred into the corridor, running over Nurse Beaulieu's big toe. He pinched her bottom in apology.

''Sorry! Just practicing my hand-eye coordination!''

''Benny Hopper! This is a hospital! Not a roller derby!'' Nurse Beaulieu favored her toe.

''10-10!'' Benny sped loose. ''Till we do it again!''

Guests soon overflowed the halls as abundantly as a pedestrian mall. Benny parked inside the shadows of the lobby. He listened to his radio with Billy the Kidney, a cerebral palsy patient. The two were as inseparable as Siamese twins whenever there was liquor stowed away in Benny's Harvey Wallbanger wheelchair.

"Here, have some more medicine," Benny proferred a Santa Claus figurine. Unscrew the red cap, and whisky poured out of Santa's head.

Billy took a swig.

"Talk about body fluids." Benny made a sour face after a sip. "You cerebral palsy sufferers look drunk, so you may as well be drunk!"

Benny and Billy evaluated the visitors who busied themselves appraising occupational therapy paintings on exhibit in the hallways.

"The philanthropists are coming! Hold up your cup! Lower your eyes!" Benny color commentated. "Where are they the other 364 days of the year? The normal people. Hale and heartless. That's what we're supposed to look like: a race of Liberaces. Here, from their Lake Placid paradise, sucking Canada Dry, we have the filthy couple Dr. and Mrs. B.S. Fuchs. A perfect 10 is not enough for Mrs. Fuchs in her shocking pink negligée for this sacred time of year. And there, fashionably late, thumping through her *grande entrée*, with her Club Med sunburn to camouflage her wino red nose, we have the bejeweled chairperson of our handicap committee, Ms. Amy Frame-Me Goody-Two-Shoes. And in the far corner, from her Morin Heights hideaway, how could we miss our one and only head nurse on her one and only night off. The old douche looks simply divine wrapped in a kimono from Woolco of tasteless green to match her yellow teeth; let us welcome the disgustingly effervescent-as-ENO ego of Nurse Phyllis Harelip. Phyllis is absolutely stunning tonight without her boxing gloves. Bluh. It hurts to watch. Talk about burlesque. Remember those stripteasers they sent over here to promote tag day? Who was teasing who? If they really wanted to offer succor, they would have let us sleep with them Chesty Morgans. Family planning. That's why charity drives always throw children at you. Chuck your local muscular dystrophy poster child under the chin. These non-profit orgs wouldn't make any money if they spread adult blobs like us all over their brochures. Because that's what those cute crippled kiddies with the cookie smiles become: big ugly Tiny Tims like us. I answered the phone once when I was living, or I should say dying, with my foster parents, Mr. Stale and Mrs. Mate. Some woman was calling with a weepy voice as if she'd been crying all night. She was requesting donations for 'Today's Disabled Youth.' I told her I've been a poor innocent disabled youth for 39 years now. Will you marry me? The forget-me-not hung up and forgot me! And what beats me is those stupid sports heroes who want to be bigger heroes. So they lay their big brother number on you, attend fund raising banquets, choke on HP sauce. And you're supposed to fall off the floor with excitement at seeing these hirsute brutes in the flesh. Like a good little Easter seal. Arp! Arp! Punch the jell-o to show them what a man you are! That's the way those hulks are conditioned to see courage. There you sit in a wheelchair like a discard from Picasso's bone period. How many of them would have the strength to endure that? Why don't the phony jocks share some of the megabucks they earn from crippling each other? Sure, be a sport. What an insult to our intelligence!''

Benny leered at Billy the Kidney. His companion had lapsed into terminal tune-out.

''You still with us?''

''... y-y-y-ye-ye-yeth...,'' Billy uttered as expressionless as a cliff face.

''Did you know that this one-armed man Pete Gray used to play outfield for the Montreal Royals at Delorimier Downs? He could burn that ball into home plate like a comet! He even made the majors with the St. Louis Browns. He could do everything except tie his own shoelaces. Runs an orphanage now in Missouri. Have to hitchhike down there some time.''

Billy shuddered kookily, not from the anecdote, but from the cold air streaming into the lobby. He hitched a ride on Benny's Harvey Wallbanger wheelchair back to warmer climes.

''When Roy Campanella wheels into Dodger Stadium the whole crowd stands up,'' Benny rambled on. ''That's the way I want it.''

Light filtered out of the sheltered workshop. A supervisor was acquainting the invitees with assorted lathes, shapers, planers, and welding tools. Nobody spotted Benny and Billy darkening the door.

''Eeep! Eeep! Want to see some sophisticated advances?'' Benny voice-activated the clinkerbox on his Harvey Wallbanger wheelchair.

Metal mobiles in the shape of dancers popped up bobbing in synch to a Cry Baby wahwah, tape loops, and fuzztones in ascending 5ths oscillating through a H&H transistor amplifier. ''Hoooeeey!'' Benny shrieked. ''I sing the body electric! 6.9 on the Richter scale!''

The sightseers stood aghast.

''I don't intend to die cranking a barrel organ in the gutter!''

''Thank you, Benny.'' The supervisor shoo'd him away.

''Nothing ever happens here.'' Benny cruised toward a pair of female legs. ''We just melt combs all day and compare bellybuttons.''

''Oh, that's nice.'' The pair of legs smiled.

''I used to take vocational training courses here to join the human race. They make you build baby coffins, chew key tags, lick envelopes. Blaaah. That's not even manual labor. That's tongue depressing! Sure, hire the handicapped. The wimps find drudgery rewarding. Incapacitate the entire workforce! Make every man and woman spineless and submissive! That'll cure our eco-spasmic economy!''

The supervisor herded the onlookers into the next room.

''See! You can't display any sign of mind here!'' Benny tapped his temporal lobe. ''They can't control that — yet! Well I'm no idiot savant! I got degrees from M.I.T. and Caltech! I didn't customize this Wallbanger out of an Erect-o set you know! This beauty is the crucible of my external soul! I've written your requisite tear-stained term papers about the plight of the handicapped, the congenital outsiders who are born then drop out of sight, those unnameables who never see the sun and whose deaths don't make the obituaries, those defective humanoids who are stigmatized in order to maintain the status quo, their need for equal opportunity and not charity, as well as enlightened legislation in regard to job discrimination, and increased public arousal concerning their sexual exigencies, and all that double shovel bull. I've studied your medical journals and research papers and books on bioethics until the books developed curvature of the spine. I'm sick of being a living, breathing, reminder of how great it must feel to have limbs. Some ignoramuses even think I'm one of those Thalidomide thingees. I have to lie to get any respect. I tell people I got fragged in Vietnam. You know how I got this way?"

"Okay Benny, enough," the supervisor stated firmly. "This isn't the time or place for that."

"I set myself on fire!" Benny's irises lit up. "I lost my parents, and my legs, in a car accident when I was a three-year-old hobbledehoy. But the older I got, the more fed up I became just sitting life out like a whoopee cushion. The world is a stage and I'm not even a walk-on.

No employer wants to hire half a body. They're looking for a man with something extra! Even though I have enough scholarships and diplomas to keep a fire blazing all night. And marriage, jeez, a jellyfish has a greater chance of finding his better half. At least a jellyfish can grow back an arm or a leg. I can't. So one fine day, guided by messianic light, I anointed myself with barbecue starter fuel, then struck a match. Boom! Like a rocket on re-entry! It took tons of Flamasene and more operations than I had fingers to calculate with to save this much of my skin, third degree burns, worse than hell. I was wrapped up for ages like a mummy in Vaseline-soaked gauze. They grafted on new skin from cadavers, sharks, cowhide, artificial flesh from plastic, everything but mother-of-pearl inlay. The rest of me they sawed off like a diseased tree. I'm a stump. For months my fever ran hotter than a radiator. My blood was black..."

"Okay, okay, chatterbox. You've had your party." The supervisor steered the Harvey Wallbanger toward the door.

"Let go!" Benny swiped at the air. "Nobody pushes me around! You make me puke with your canned tears! I'm going to the toilet to commit suicide!"

Billy the Kidney doddered after Benny. Benny pressed the "up" button on the self-service elevator. Their bodies went up, their insides went down. The walls of the second floor opened their gray wings. The floors were as shiny as a shuffleboard court. Well-wishers roamed through the offices. Their mirth echoed off concrete, gypsum, and glass. In the physiotherapy room, a paralytic woman was demonstrating the use of pulleys, weights, and latbars.

''We found her at last! The ugliest girl in Canada!'' Benny crooned into the room. ''Forget it, Rubella! The best part of you ran down your daddy's leg!''

All eyes about-faced.

''Don't mind us, folks. We're just bionic freaks.''

''Stop calling me Rubella!'' Ella Finestedt converged upon Benny with the cold eye of a locomotive. She attacked his Harvey Wallbanger wheelchair with her crutches.

''Okay, bitch!'' He rolled himself into a ball. ''Some women put flowers in their hair. She puts spiders!''

''Benny! You're obnoxious!'' Nurse Beaulieu separated the two combatants.

''I'm obnoxious? She's obnoxious! I ought to have that vulgar virgin arrested for assaulting my batteries!''

''Don't play your silly facetious games with me you! Apologize to Ella this minute!''

''Drop dead.''

''Benny!''

''Alright, alright. Mercy, mercy. Ella, I lust for your bust, wherever it may be. I crave to undress you with my teeth. You are the thorny rose amongst the vegetables here.''

Tears of rage slalomed down Ella's cheeks. She clamped her eyes shut and clomped out of the room. Her prosthetic leg dipped like a plunger. The hush of the spectators intensified the scraping sound.

''Well, Benny Hopper! Are you happy now?'' Nurse Beaulieu vented her spleen.

''Oh, Ella hates people anyways— especially men. They always laugh at her leg.'' Benny swerved into the hallway. ''Remember last year she didn't want anybody to be in her photographs while she took snapshots of the Christmas tree, and the cake, and the table leg.''

Benny left the room, Billy the Kidney in pursuit.

Benny could feel the music downstairs through his wheelchair.

''Good, good, good vibrations.'' He snapped his two fingers funkily in the elevator.

''Have mercy! Live music this year!'' Benny scooted into the banquet hall. He collided with an orderly.

''Ow! Benny! Watch where you aim that tank!'' The orderly massaged his ankle.

''It's okay. I took out the rocket launcher.''

''I'll probably be sorry for asking, but are you enjoying yourself?''

''Listen. Not counting the rush from riding the onanism express every morning, my heart is hotter and more positively charged with absolute bliss than the glow of an RCA 6CW4 vacuum tube which is what my viscera feel like in there empowering this unequivocally saltant high never before scaled in human history since that incompetent and impotent new male nurse accidentally mixed up his Speedballs with my Sopors as a dopamine balancer while the hellish helix of my DNA mutated a wee interfaith trickster that steeplechased over theophysical obstacles in my anthropocephalon with buckets of holy Perrier to put out the St. Elmo's fire sizzling and scrolling my rocoocoo neurotransmitters zugzwanged by the Cherry Rum Fix relaying eudemonic pictorial essays to that sempiternal playgirl Alice in Wonderland who delivered the *kyrie eleison* back into the spirit world!''

''I knew you'd say that.''

''Good thing you finally scrapped that arrhythmic record player. The one that always skipped unless you put a quarter on its arm. Figures. Even the turntables around here need a new arm unit.''

The hour arrived to announce the winner of the Yuletide Writing Festival: Natasha Borenson, a cystic fibrosis patient, for her piece ''A Gift of Dark Horses.'' Her story was about how animals cannot distinguish if a human being is deformed or not, and if only people could be that way. Natasha was honored with a cash prize more generous than her allowance, plus a box of chocolates. She was shy about her lungs. So her mother recited the two-page composition.

''Yucky, yucky. So that's the kind of sugar-coated shit they wanted for their O Henry chocolate bar award!'' Benny bit the arm rest of his wheelchair. ''I preferred it when they used to just show us Nativity scenes on a slide projector. I knew my poem wouldn't win. I told it like it is. Want to hear?''

Billy the Kidney nodded neutrally.

''Okay. What's it feel like to be a freak? Like vegetating inside a bubble watching Gilligan's Island for the rest of your life. Like a phylogenetic drop-out beneath all the plebeians. Like Ironsides in quicksand. Don't give us charity, all you Jerry Lewis dubbies. It just goes into the salary of our body snatchers, and afflicts the secretary with paperalysis. You can't walk tall in a wheelchair with only Medicare to care. So up yours, and kiss mine. Merry Christmas!''

Billy the Kidney continued to read the spots in his eyes.

''Well? Don't just stand there like a bobbing head doll. Say something!''

Nothing.

''Come on, spit it out! You're not in a classroom!''

''... g-g-g-g-g-g-goo-goo-goo-good,'' Billy stuttered with a cervical wobble.

''That's easy for you to say.'' Benny sniggered. ''I'm starting to like poetry. Have mercy. Milton was blind. Keats was consumptive. Byron had a club foot. And Homer was a hundred people in one: the worst-case multiple personality in all of tragedy! Cripes! The ancients magnified their monsters into myths. We get purged under a microscope!''

A volunteer catered to them with snacks. Benny fondled a peach.

''Forbidden fruit?''

''Go ahead. Take one.''

''I'll bet you Sigmund Freud's wet couch that these peaches are analphobic and wish to return to the womb!''

''You're a smart one aren't you? You could at least say thank you.''

''For what?''

''Well, peaches are fairly expensive this time of year. There are people out there less fortunate than you and I who would envy a meal like this and...''

''Want to trade places?''

''If you don't appreciate the food then put it back.''

''Up yours!'' Benny gobbled a sandwich wedge, cheeks bulging like chipmunk pouches. ''And while you're on your feet, could you fetch me some punch?''

''Fetch it yourself!'' The volunteer left in a huff.

''These bloody tuna sandwiches are rancid, and crawling with bugs, and should be tossed back into the sea!'' He spluttered after her, spraying Billy with morsels.

Benny was becoming too audible, louder than the band.

''Coocooroocoocoo! Chiba-chiba! Ayeee!

Ayeee!'' Benny clapped with one hand. ''Come on you blow jobs! Play some music! This isn't a mortuary!''

The holiday cuisine shushed Benny up, temporarily. The main course was spare ribs. Poinsettias rested beside the plates of female patients. After sponge cake and ice cream, the dance floor opened up to anyone who could still move. A corps of convalescents swung their hips slower than the beat. Oooh's and aaah's accompanied every sitzspin.

Billy rode shotgun with Benny to the punchbowl. ''Mr. Hopper! Don't get drunk!'' A thick French accent commanded.

''Léo! *Mon pite!*'' Benny reached out to shake fingers with his blind friend, Léo Laflamme. ''I haven't laid eyes on you since those stripteasers came down here to raise our moneymakers!''

''I 'ear you everywhere wid your big mouth. You're back?''

''Naturally, *beaucoup de booboos.*''

''How you mean? Booboos?''

''Oh, just booboos, you know: doctors, lawyers, caseworkers, chaplains. At least the Greek cook doesn't make the sign of the cross anymore when she sees me coming.''

''I don't unnerstand?''

''Forget it. Tonight I just came to kiss the nurses.''

''*Eh ben*, me too!'' Léo lifted his dark glasses and winked a blind eye.

"They won't let me be Santa Claus this year."

"Cuz you drink too much."

"Is it my fault they dump too much alcool into the punch?"

"Don't drink. Dat's all."

"Why shouldn't I? I don't drive."

"Da band she's good, han?" Léo changed the subject.

"Black ties, white shirts, cheap frills, Stevie Wonder roll over."

"Dey don't make you feel joy?"

"Joy who? Joy detergent? Is there a Joy in the house? I'll feel her!"

Benny was too gauche for Léo. Benny couldn't see eye-to-eye with anyone, blind or sighted. He and Léo parted paths beside the cold cuts.

"All wrecks aboard!" Benny gave the high sign to Billy the Kidney, "Let's go to the john for some real juice. This punch tastes like water on the knee."

Rolling thunder, the duo crashed into the washroom door. A stranger was relieving himself.

"Hey mister! Have a game of craps? We're wandering scholars."

The stranger zippered up his pants, then tore off.

Benny groped for the Santa Claus figurine in his portable bar. He untwisted the red cap with his teeth.

''I should have been a bartender.'' Whiskey dribbled down his chin onto his sweater. ''Another shot of this and you'll be running around the block backwards. I'm drinking mine straight from the jug. I don't want any of your cerebral palsy germs.''

Billy bolted down the scotch in one spastic gulp. He began to cough uncontrollably.

''Here.'' Benny scooped up some slush off the floor and blended it into another drink. ''Madhouse Mist.''

Billy braced himself against the wall as if in zero gravity. He downed the pick-me-up, then capsized to the floor.

''Roll them bones!'' Benny cast a pair of dice onto the tiles.

The dice scattered like white mice under a cubicle.

''Sick 'em, dogbreath!''

Billy let his fingers do the walking toward the dice.

''Hurry up before the paint peels from your breath!''

Billy scudded back, drooling saliva.

''Maybe I should just attach a tube to your nostrils and let this weapons-grade whiskey disintegrate the undevastated regions of your cortical debris?'' Benny re-filled another Santa cap.

Again the sting caused Billy to cough.

''*Gesundheit! Gesundheit!*'' Benny whacked Billy on each buttock. ''Say! That reminds me! Want to see what I got myself for Christmas?''

Benny stole into the depths of his Harvey Wallbanger wheelchair. He extracted a German luger. The metal gleamed like a knife.

''Sharp, eh?''

Billy didn't twitch a muscle.

''Guess how many crippled-kiddie-loving hypocrites we could knock off with this baby?'' Benny poised the gun upright on its stock.

''See! Stands up straighter than you or I ever will!''

Billy lay flat as a mat.

''Ever hear of mercy killing?'' Benny aimed the barrel at Billy's damaged brain.

Dead silence.

''I don't mean you. I mean *them*. They're the ones I feel sorry for.''

Benny fidgeted with the firing pin. He drew a bead on himself in the mirror.

'' You dare me?''

Billy lay blotto.

Benny hugged the gun against his breastbone.

''My death won't diminish anyone.''

His eyes flinched tighter as he squeezed the trigger harder. Nurse Beaulieu barged in.

''Benny! What...''

The lugerblast exploded like a thunderclap. Billy stirred, covered with mirror shards. A bull's eye stared back where Benny's image had been.

''You're going to pay for this!'' Nurse

Beaulieu blanched. ''What's wrong with Billy?''

''Oh, the retard can't walk upright without a hockey helmet.''

Guests and personnel flooded into the washroom. Kierkegaard confiscated the luger.

''Benny you're not making sense!'' Nurse Beaulieu flew into conniptions. ''You're not stable! You're not rational! You're not coherent!''

''I'm epiphenomenal.''

''Oooo! Sometimes I feel like shaking that sick brain of yours . . . .''

''I don't need any doctors, MD's, meat dealers.''

''We'll see about that!''

Dr. Overbye spread out the spanking new Santa costume across his desk. The previous Father Christmas had outfatted the old suit. Its hindquarters had been hobo-stitched with scarlet, yellow, and blue patches. This unworn ladies auxiliary special came equipped with a black belt, silver buckle, white fur trim, and a matching beard. The real goods.

''Well, Benny. We have a surprise for you. We've decided to let you be Santa Claus.''

Benny feasted his good eye on the winterwear, suspicious of the reverse psychology.

''What gives?''

''Nurse Grosseteste's husband has the flu. So we decided to be different this year and have one of the patient's act as Santa. You, my friend, are The Chosen One. But before you commute over any rooftops, we'd appreciate it if you took two of these tranquilizers."

"I knew there was a catch!"

"No catch, Benny. We just don't want you fainting on us like last year's Santa."

"Sorry, doc." Benny filliped the Libriums into a corner. "My stomach is full of punch anyway."

"You can wait an hour and then take these, or else we simply ring up Alaska for our usual standby. What do you say?"

Benny mistrusted Dr. Overbye's deskside manner, his droll professionalism. He stroked the fur collar without any sensation in his fingertips. But to fit inside these happy integuments would restore a sensitivity in him beyond synthetic touch.

"Have mercy. I'll do it!"

"Good show!"

Nurse Beaulieu assisted Benny into the Santa ensemble. A safety pin here, a bobby pin there, nip and tuck, Old Saint Nick himself would have mistaken Benny for a mirror image. Tinsel and candy cane streamers substituted for the baseball cards and baby booties on the Harvey Wallbanger wheelchair.

"You're the skinniest Santa we've ever had." Dr. Overbye jabbed Benny in the solar plexis. "Want another pillow?"

"Got two in there already, doc! I'm more wrapped up than the presents!"

The beard hooked on askew. The cotton bush swaddled his entire anatomy. Benny possessed solely one outer ear. The pinna and lobe of the other had been seared off in his suicide attempt.

"You look Satanic," Nurse Beaulieu sized him up.

"Just hitch up the reindeer to my Harvey Wallbanger and come fly with me!"

"You're not nervous?"

"Me? Nervous? No. I was an Episcopalian butterfly squished by a monk on a bicycle during an earlier incarnation."

"How's your French?" Dr. Overbye queried.

"My French? Sounds like an ailment. I pledge allegiance to altered states. *Je me souviens.*"

"Just give out the gifts, Benny. That'll say everything."

"Into the chimney we go!" Nurse Beaulieu chauffeured Benny into the elevator.

"Hope I don't get burned again."

"Benny, you are about to be roasted to perfection!"

They hit the ground floor. Female volunteers swarmed around Benny like groupies. The band had been playing "Here Comes Santa" for twenty minutes. Had Benny had any legs, they would have been trembling. He was paraded into the banquet hall with as much pomp as royalty on horseback.

"*C'est* Benny! *C'est Père Noël!*"

Benny forgot to ho-ho, silenced by the cheers.

"When we want you to be quiet, you talk like a crazy mouth." Nurse Beaulieu willy-weaved him around the dining tables. "And when we want you to talk, you shut up!"

Benny forced out a "ho-ho," louder, then louder, and louder, until one with the din. The laughter was infectious. He popped a wheelie with his Harvey Wallbanger wheelchair.

"My phantom limbs are boogie-woogying in heaven!" Benny's good and bad eye sparkled as brightly as the Christmas lights.

The hospital staff lent a hand in distributing the gifts. Natasha Borenson was the first pick again.

"I don't think there's any dark horses in here." Benny jiggled a miniature box tied with a blue ribbon.

Ella Finestedt's moment arrived. She was still upset over Benny's posturizing in the physiotherapy room.

"Why didn't you carry the bag on your head? Bozo!"

"I should have! Like a model in the Toulouse-Lautrec Finishing School!" Benny would never lose his funny bone.

Ella bent over to seize her present. Benny planted a kiss on her chin.

"Ow! That hurt! What was that for?"

"Oh, just a personal token of my affection.

I'm, ah, thinking of connecting a sidecar to this wheelchair, a... ummm... love seat."

"A what?"

"I have audiocassettes of Barbara Streisand and Twisted Sister. We could go up to the mountain in summer and watch the fireworks. I'll protect you from the muggers. This Wallbanger is strong enough for two people. We won't have to wait for excursions on the Good Samaritan bus with the others. I don't have AIDS you know. You can touch me."

Benny extended his two fingers in forgiveness.

"Well?"

"Well..." Ella gripped her crutches.

"Catch you in physiotherapy?"

"Okay." Ella squeezed his two fingers. "Come up and see me sometime."

"Have mercy!"

The biggest box under the tree was reserved for Billy the Kidney. Benny shook its contents to test if they were liquid. Nope. Alcohol doesn't rattle.

"Th-th-th-th-th-than-than-than-thank y-y-y-y-y-you!" Billy jigabood off, all ribbons and smiles.

"That's easy for you to say!" The hospital laughed with Benny.

Fair shakes ensued with a conga line of dancing wheelchairs. They bopped like bumper cars — the only recorded cases of whiplash from waltzing! All forms of pain and loneliness danced as merrily as dimes. Benny strummed a guitar with his right hand while the bandleader synchronized the chord changes with his left. Loud and mute voices sang "All You Need Is Love."

Santa beard dangling from his one ear, Benny's Harvey Wallbanger wheelchair was lowered off the stage.

"Well, Dr. Overbye! What do you think of my motor skills now?"

"Genius finds a way, Benny. I'm glad you got your motivation back."

"Thanks for stopping the world and letting me on!"

"What?" Dr. Overbye cocked an incredulous ear. "What's that I heard you say? Thank you?"

"Yes." Benny's eyes danced. "Thank you. Thank you very much."

Printed by
the workers of
Ateliers Graphiques Marc Veilleux Inc.
Cap-Saint-Ignace, Qué.